"You've got this all wrong!"

Emma's voice croaked as she almost managed to start breathing properly again. Even as she spoke, she was vibrantly conscious of Brick's proximity.

"Look," she went on, finally accepting that he was no airy figment of her imagination. He was a real-live, pulsating, knee-buckling, flesh-and-blood male. "It doesn't make sense. Why don't you let me go so I can—" she paused "—so I can sort of start to *breathe* again?"

Brick's arms tightened around her waist, and she could feel her breasts rising and falling rapidly against his muscular chest.

"Your breathing," he murmured just above her lips, "leaves nothing to be desired!"

SALLY HEYWOOD is a British author, born in Yorkshire.
After leaving university, she had several jobs, including
running an art gallery, a guest house and a boutique. She
has written several plays for theater and television, in
addition to her romance novels for Harlequin. Her special
interests are sailing, reading, fashion, interior decorating
and helping in a children's nursery.

Books by Sally Heywood

HARLEQUIN PRESENTS

HARLEQUIN ROMANCE

Don't miss any of our special offers. Write to us at the
following address for information on our newest releases.

Harlequin Reader Service
P.O. Box 1397, Buffalo, NY 14240
Canadian address: P.O. Box 603,
Fort Erie, Ont. L2A 5X3

SALLY HEYWOOD

the gemini bride

Harlequin Books

TORONTO • NEW YORK • LONDON
AMSTERDAM • PARIS • SYDNEY • HAMBURG
STOCKHOLM • ATHENS • TOKYO • MILAN
MADRID • WARSAW • BUDAPEST • AUCKLAND

Harlequin Presents first edition June 1992
ISBN 0-373-11466-4

Original hardcover edition published in 1990
by Mills & Boon Limited

THE GEMINI BRIDE

CHAPTER ONE

RAIN was slashing at the high windows as if intent on forcing its way into the room. For the last twenty minutes Emma had felt like somebody on board a storm-bound ship, waiting for the final grinding moment as it hit rock.

She smiled to herself. Her imagination! The reality was quite different. Here she was sitting in Lady Burley's library cataloguing some priceless leather-bound volumes, earning her daily bread! The only thing to do with ships and shipwrecks, apart from the storm raging over London at this moment, were the crackling pages of the diaries she had just catalogued— diaries of one of Lady Burley's swashbuckling ances-tors, a seventeenth-century admiral, but in Emma's eyes more like a pirate if his amazing exploits were to be believed!

She gazed dreamily into the embers of the log fire for a moment and wondered if Octavius Burley had looked as wicked as he sounded. His diaries would have made her blush if she were the blushing type and she pulled herself up, remembering she was supposed to be cataloguing the books, not reading them!

Apart from him, and the rain—she looked round the room—there was nothing ship-like about her present surroundings at all. It was as rosy as an elegant eighteenth-century mansion in Belgravia could be. Three walls were covered in glass-fronted cupboards within which were shelf after shelf of leather-bound books, gold titles gleaming richly in the light from the green-shaded brass lamp beside her.

Then there was a most unshiplike Aubusson under-
foot, a spectacular cut crystal chandelier drooping from
a heavily moulded ceiling, and a group of comfortable
armchairs built for curling up in with a good book, all
covered in red velvet and heaped with a rainbow
assortment of coloured silk cushions.

'What a heavenly room!' she had exclaimed when
Lady Burley had shown her into it three weeks
previously.

The older woman, gaunt and excessively chic, had
smiled with pleasure. 'Your enthusiasm is most encour-
aging, my dear. I hope it means you'll last longer than
the previous gel!'

Emma had felt like a fool, showing her admiration
so openly. But then, what was the use of pretending?
she asked herself. She had never guessed people like
Lady Burley existed outside the pages of glossy magazines and the whole house was like something in a
photograph. Previously Belgravia had been merely a
name. Now she understood that the brief glimpses of
chauffeur-driven limousines sailing grandly about the
streets of London carried real live people, not the
inventions of some adman in an ivory tower. She hadn't
come to terms with the situation at all. Meanwhile, she
thanked her lucky stars that 'the previous gel' had
decided to run off and get married, leaving this peach
of a job to turn up at just the right time for Emma
Andrews!

The oak-panelled door behind her whispered open,
bringing her back to the present with a start. The
butler, Mr Heaton, or Jack as he'd asked her to call
him, poked his head round, asking in most unbutlerlike
tones, 'Want another coffee, Emma?'

She raised her fair head from the book that lay open
at its title page, adjusting to reality with a little blink

of her blue eyes. She gave him a vague smile. 'That would be lovely, Jack. But I'm going to have to dash out to the post as soon as this rain stops.'

'Anything we can deal with?'

'No, thanks. I have to choose a birthday card for a friend.'

'Very well.'

She giggled. 'Now you sound exactly like a butler!'

He put on a poker face and glided into the room. 'Anything further, madam?'

'Stop it, you idiot. I don't know how you manage to keep a straight face when Lady Burley's entertaining!'

'One does one's best, ma'am.' He bowed, then gave her a sidelong grin. 'Seriously, I've got to send the boy out on an errand. He can choose a card and pop it in the post for you if you tell me what you want.'

'You are sweet, Jack, but no. It's the sort of job I like to do myself. Besides, I'm getting on quite well here and deserve a short break!'

'OK, coffee coming up.' He peered out of the window before he left. 'Take my umbrella at least. It's blowing up a proper storm.'

After he'd gone out, she gave a little smile. She had always thought butlers, if indeed they existed in this day and age, were around seventy. Jack had been a bit of a shock for he couldn't be more than twenty-eight.

Emma frowned, her heart-shaped face reflecting every thought that flitted through her mind. It must be nice, she was thinking, to have a training and a job. After she had finished here she would have to think of getting some proper training herself. The trouble was that she didn't know what she wanted to do. When Olga had died she had left home without thinking things through, using her small inheritance to see something of the world and to put a distance between her old life and the new one she felt was just about to open up.

That had all been very well, but now, back in London, she suddenly realised she was completely alone, with nothing and no one she could call her own. At least if she learned to *do* something she would have something to offer.

She sucked the end of her pencil, her concentration broken by Jack's interruption. Apart from travelling and going around in an aimless sort of way, all she'd done since leaving school was work in Olga's little wool shop in the small Suffolk town where she had been brought up.

She hadn't been able to leave Olga so soon after Edwin's death, and one year had stretched into another until before she knew it she was twenty-one and it seemed too late to think of going to college. Then Olga had died and she was still trying to sort out the jumble her life seemed to have become.

What she really liked was rooting around in old books, ferreting out odd pieces of information, putting things in order. Not, she sighed, enough to build a life on, surely?

She gently closed the volume in front of her and went over to the window with an assessing look in her eye. Yes, the rain had definitely eased if it hadn't exactly stopped, and with Jack's big black umbrella it would be nice to splash across the square to the shops. A girl could have too much of sitting indoors!

She went into the cool white and eau-de-Nil foyer—it was too grand to call it a hallway—and, clicking over the marble floor in her high heels, reached the top of the stairs leading down to Jack's lair. She rang the bell, and when he curled his head round the edge of the door at the bottom she said, 'I'll have that coffee later. I'll slip out now. I've just finished the Qs.'

Grinning, he disappeared and returned almost at once. 'Take this.' He handed her his umbrella then gave her a critical examination. 'You're not going out in those shoes, are you?' He eyed her court shoes, then, as if he couldn't help it, she saw his eyes slide over her ankles and up her legs to the hem of her skirt.

Annoyed, she said, 'Don't cosset, Jack. I'm not made of porcelain!'

'I can see that!' he quipped, taking in the waist-length blonde hair and the peaches and cream complexion. 'I can see that all too well. . .You're much nicer!' He gave a sort of friendly leer and she swivelled sharply to show him he'd gone too far. Briskly she donned her coat then made her way to the main door and let herself out.

By the time she reached the bookshop on the main road she was angrily aware that at least he had been right to criticise her for not borrowing a pair of boots. Her feet were soaking and the backs of her legs were splashed with mud. Running into the shelter of the store, she rapidly chose a card, queued impatiently at the cash desk then made her way to the exit and stood poised for a moment under the awning outside, preparing to make a dash back through the rain to the house. She had been wrong to imagine the slight easing off in the weather meant that the storm was over. If anything it was worse.

She pulled the collar of her coat tighter around her neck and was just about to plunge off into the street again when there was a shout behind her and a hand came down on to her shoulder, pivoting her as she lifted her head.

'I can't believe it! What on earth are you doing *here*?'

She felt a star-burst of a smile envelop her, then she was being pulled, a tangle of long fair hair and wet coat, into the arms of a complete stranger.

'Hey! *Let me go!*' She raised her head, expecting the man to release her at once when he realised his mistake, but instead he more thoroughly enveloped her and her protests were cut off as she became breathlessly aware of his hard-packed muscles moulding her against him. It seemed flagrantly intimate and so unexpected she could only wilt in his arms as her eyes widened in an effort to get to grips with the situation.

She wasn't even breathing, she noted peripherally, her eyes skidding back and forth over the handsome, strong-lined face smiling down into her own. Two short black brows drew attention to the glittering hazel eyes. A straight, determined-looking nose led the glance inevitably to a pair of lips that, even now, as she felt herself beginning to droop in his arms, were hovering within kissing distance. And they were lips, she noted, made entirely for kissing. . .

As she blinked with a half-formed idea that the man was an emanation of her own imagination due to too much reading about pirates that morning, his own eyes were lapping over her face in a mixture of pleasure and something else, something, she registered, much less friendly. She gave a shiver and wondered what it meant.

'*Well*?' He shook her impatiently as shoppers surged on both sides of them. 'No excuses? No explanations? It's not like you to be stuck for a story! You realise we've been combing the country for you? Sybil thought you'd gone up to Scotland. But I said no, she'll stick around where the action is. But I never guessed you'd be so close to home. Or are you just on your way back?'

'Look,' she croaked, when she almost managed to start breathing properly again, 'you've got this all wrong.' Even as she spoke she was vibrantly conscious of the man's continuing proximity, aware now that he was no airy figment of the imagination but a real-life, pulsating, knee-buckling, flesh and blood male. 'Look,' she repeated confusedly, 'I don't know what you're talking about. It doesn't make sense. But why don't you just let me go so I can——' she paused '—so I can sort of start to *breathe* again?'

His arms tightened around her waist and she could feel her breasts rising and falling rapidly against his muscular chest.

'Your breathing,' he murmured just above her lips, 'leaves nothing to be desired.'

She was mesmerised by his lips as they drew back in a mirthless smile. His teeth, she registered dreamily, were too perfect. Simply beautiful. Why had she never noticed what miraculous things teeth were? They were so white, so even, so. . .so strong-looking.

'Look. . .' She pulled herself together and began to make a token attempt at getting away from such heaven. 'Pleasant though this is, I'd rather you backed off a little. OK?' She grinned despite herself because it was impossible to be offended by such a gorgeous beast. Given the choice she would stay in his arms like this all day! 'I don't know you. . .unfortunately,' she went on—regaining some of her self-possession—'but I really don't think you should behave like this in public!'

Her words seemed to shock him into slackening his grip and she managed to slither out of his arms, though he adjusted his hold so she was tethered to him by the ends of her mackintosh belt. They stood like that for an endless moment, swaying a little as shoppers continued to flow around them.

'I like the accent,' he told her, head on one side, a judging, half-amused, half-angry look in his eyes.

For the first time she registered that he wasn't English. A fleeting image of wide open spaces dazzled her. He would look marvellous on horseback. Riding into town. A neckerchief at his throat. Leather boots. Spurs jangling. The theme from *The Big Country* filling the movie theatre.

She gave a gasp of annoyance, partly directed at herself, and yanked the belt of her coat free from out of his grasp. He hadn't been holding it as tightly as she thought. Then she stepped back, drawing herself up and giving him one of her haughtiest stares. 'It's been *so* nice meeting you! Sorry I have to go!'

She swivelled and at once found herself being borne away in the eddying crowd. When she shot a look back over her shoulder his head was thrown back in a laugh of pure delight. 'Perfect!' he called over the milling heads. 'You've obviously been doing some homework! See you Thursday!'

His smile stayed with her as she slipped out into the rain.

When she turned for a last glimpse he was staring after her, smile just beginning to fade. He shook his head at her when their eyes met. 'Make the most of your freedom, sweetheart!' he called. 'Start Thursday. Don't you dare forget!' He gave a last sardonic lift of his eyebrows and then, as if he didn't trust her, he fixed her with a blazing glance, his eyes boring into hers, daring her to disobey. It took all her determination to turn away. It was the look more than his words that made her clench her fists. He made her feel about two feet high! What an arrogant devil! she thought furiously. Whoever he thought I was, I'm glad I'm not!

She ran all the way back to the house in the square under Jack's umbrella, throwing herself up the front steps and into the porch with its two white Doric columns on either side, feeling as if she was unable to trust herself to linger in streets with a man like that on the loose, and when she pressed her finger on the bell it was like summoning help.

He had made her feel weak, vulnerable, helpless. . .and lots of other things she had never felt before. It was ridiculous!

'Phew!' she exclaimed when Jack came to let her in, 'Must have a look at my horoscope today! I've just had a most peculiar encounter with a tall, dark stranger!' And she told him all about it as she shook out the umbrella, peeled off her tights in the maid's pantry, and stuffed newspapers into her leather shoes before placing them side by side on the Aga. 'I wonder who he thought I was,' she finished up. 'Poor girl! I hope she doesn't mind dancing to *his* tune!'

'Would you?' asked Jack humorously. 'Not 'alf by the sound of things!' He looked rather put out.

Emma flashed him a smile. 'I hope *he* didn't think so! I'd hate to add to his conceit. He obviously likes to have the whip hand!'

She gave a mock shudder and it turned itself into a real one as she remembered the last warning words he had thrown at her. There was something urgent and dangerous about him, even though he had been quite affable on the surface. She began to wonder about him as she settled back to work, and by the end of the afternoon she had gone over every little detail her startled senses had been able to record.

* * *

'About thirtyish. Tall, rangy-looking. That cowboy accent!'

'What was he wearing?'

She frowned. 'Very casual gear. Almost thrown on. As if he was in a tearing hurry. But beautiful. Rich, deep, masculine colours. I think he wore a sweater in kind of dark reds and deep blues. . . I put my hand up to ward him off and I felt soft wool. . .' She closed her eyes for a moment, reliving the rich, deep warmth of him.

'Cashmere?' Judy, the girl from the bedsit across the landing, leaned forward, breaking into her daydream.

'I don't know.' Emma opened her eyes and gave her a glancing smile. 'Does it matter? We'll never meet again. It was just one of those things——' She pulled a face.

'Just one of those wonderful things,' sang Judy under her breath. She was smiling. 'The least I can do is read your chart for you!'

Emma gave her a sceptical glance then hastily covered it with an apologetic shrug. 'I can't make myself believe the stars would bother to predict a one-off meeting. Though it sure feels as if they should!' She looped her long, waist-length hair round one hand and fiddled about with it on top of her head. It was almost dry from the wetting she had got on her way home, and Judy had brought over a hairdrier for her to borrow. It was then her story about her afternoon's brief encounter had come spilling out.

'It would show up if you were going to have a big romance this year,' suggested Judy with a serious frown. She wasn't put out by Emma's scepticism. Instead her eyes sparkled with interest. 'I don't know whether it works or how it works. But it's fun to do. All I need is your place, date and time of birth. Most people don't know the exact time but an approximation will do——'

'I know the exact time. It's written on my birth certificate.' Emma went over to the bedside table where she kept all her important bits and pieces, and extracted her birth certificate from where she kept it inside her passport. 'There you are.' She handed it over. 'Do your worst.'

'I thought your name was Andrews?' asked Judy, scanning the document.

'I was adopted at birth. I've used the name of the people I finally ended up with since I was fourteen. Olga and Edwin Andrews,' she explained. 'It was Olga who died last year and left me some money. Her husband, my adoptive dad, died five years ago. They were both quite elderly. Done a lot of fostering, and I was their last one.' She grinned. 'I was lucky. I got their undivided attention!'

Judy didn't say anything. Instead she reached for a pencil and jotted down the details. 'Emma's date,' she said with a flourish. 'I'll run it through the computer straight away while you finish drying your hair. Be back in a while.' She got up. 'Come through and help me set up the programme if you like.'

'Won't I jinx the mechanism? You know I don't believe in astrology!'

'I don't think it'll care one bit!'

When Judy went out Emma rummaged around for a hairbrush, then thoughtfully untangled her long, silky tresses with one hand while wafting the drier over them with the other.

'All right, Madame Arcate!' she exclaimed as she breezed into Judy's room half an hour later. 'What does the mysterious future hold? And when and where am I going to meet my handsome, dark-haired stranger again?'

Judy looked up with wide eyes. 'Not so fast, Emma. This is interesting. I'd hate to get it wrong and raise false hopes. . .'

Emma gave a mocking laugh and flopped down into the saggy old armchair on the other side of Judy's gas fire. 'I'm all ears,' she replied. 'Ready when you are!'

It was because of what Judy had told her that she left the mansion block next morning with a buoyant step. It was nice to be told pleasant things—even if they weren't likely to turn out to be true! Judy was a card. What with her talk of dark-haired strangers, she was hardly original, though she had the air of one who really knew what she was talking about. Emma had to give her that.

'I didn't realise you could do evening classes in astrology,' she had murmured when Judy had enlarged on the reading they had pieced together out of a sheaf of photocopied lecture notes.

'I'm only a beginner,' she explained. 'This is only my second year.'

'Goodness!' exclaimed Emma, feeling she ought to keep her humorous comments to herself in future.

Now, as she hurried through the rush-hour crowds towards the Tube, she grinned at the thought of what lay ahead—*if* Judy were to be believed!

'But I don't want a complete change of fortune!' she had protested last night. 'I think I'm very fortunate as I am! It was a real stroke of luck landing the job I've got. If I hadn't knocked that sheaf of magazines down in the bookstore I would never have read the adverts on the back page and never read the job vacancies. I call that fortunate enough for anybody! Besides, I really like cataloguing Lady Burley's family library. It might seem dull to some people, but I love it. I can really let my imagination go!'

'What happens when the job's done?' Judy had asked mildly.

Emma had curled her nose. 'Heavens, that's *weeks* into the future!'

'You really are footloose! What about settling down?' Judy had glanced hurriedly at the scribbled notes in front of her.

'Is that written?' Emma had eyed the notes upside-down. They'd made as much sense to her that way as right side up.

'Not exactly. You're going to travel across wide seas to foreign lands. But you're going *to* someone. There's a marriage here.'

'A *marriage*? Mine, you mean?'

Judy had frowned. 'You'll have to let me work it out carefully. I might even take it to class with me. If you don't mind?' She'd looked up.

Emma had laughed. 'How flattering! What if they discover something dreadful? Will you promise to tell me?'

Judy had smiled confidently. 'I can assure you of one thing, Emma, you're going to have an absolutely wonderful life. That much is certain. See here. . .' and she'd come out with a lot of jargon that had left Emma feeling confused but happy.

'It's as good as a tonic to hear all this,' she had said contentedly.

And the tonic lasted most of the morning. Round about lunchtime she stood up and went over to the window to look down into the square. The trees behind the iron railings were bare now. It would be pretty in summer with the lawns and the flower-beds and the

wooden summerhouse beneath its arch of green willow.
She wondered if she would still be here. Judy said not.
She rather hoped she was wrong. She quite liked it
here, though she felt in her bones she would eventually
move on.

There was a row of parking meters along the kerb,
each of the spaces occupied by an impressive-looking
car. One or two passers-by hurried along the pavement.
The sun was filtering weakly through scudding grey
clouds. She debated whether to go out or not. Jack
would bring her lunch up on a tray if she wanted, or
she could eat with the kitchen staff. So far she had
avoided that, feeling that the young butler would take
it as a sign he had a chance.

What Judy had said about marriage amused her. She
had no intention of getting married. Now she was free
she didn't plan on staying anywhere long enough to
make that sort of commitment. It would be nice, she
mused. But marrying and setting up home was something other people did.

She didn't belong anywhere. She never had done. It
was too much even for *her* imagination to believe
things would ever change. Knowing she didn't belong
made her wary of any involvement. Besides, making
ends meet took up all her time these days. Maybe she
had been foolish to blow all the money Olga had left
her on travel, but it had seemed too little to do anything
serious with and a house was the last thing she had
wanted to put it on, even a tiny one. She had wanted
to see the world.

With a little shrug of impatience she went towards
the door. Maybe it wasn't good to work alone like a
monk in a cell? She was becoming quite introspective
in her old age!

Without seeing anyone she stepped outside into the

watery sunshine. A stiff breeze blew her long hair in fronds around her face. With a little laugh of sheer high spirits she ran lightly down the steps towards the pavement. . .and slap bang into the arms of a man who just at that moment swung in towards the steps.

She gave a gasp and almost fell. '*You*! What are *you* doing here?' she managed to croak.

'Thought you were being clever, didn't you?' drawled the same dark-haired stranger she had encountered in the shop yesterday. 'You crazy idiot!' he went on. 'You should have known there'd be a full-scale council of war when I got back. Now they've sent me to get you!'

'*What*?' She stepped back, bumping into the bottom of the steps. At least he hadn't taken her in his arms again. It should have made the task of making sense of the situation easier. But it didn't. 'How did you know where I was?' she asked faintly.

'Followed you yesterday, of course. As you ran off into the rain it suddenly occurred to me that if you were going to do your disappearing act again I'd be kicking myself for letting you go. So I followed you. And you were so sure of yourself, you didn't even look back!'

'Why the hell should I?' Something in the arrogant assumption that he'd got the better of her made her draw herself up and treat him to an icy glance. 'I'm not accustomed to being followed about the streets like a police suspect, actually.'

'*Actually? You aren't*?' he mimicked her English accent. Then his voice became toe-curlingly North American again as he drawled, 'Look here, sweetheart, this has gone far enough. I have to hand it to you, you've done a pretty good job of covering your tracks, but all good things come to an end, as they say. And this is it. *The end.*'

She concealed a shiver. What he was saying was nothing to do with her, thank goodness. She gave him a sarcastically polite smile. 'Do you always talk in this, how shall we say, this gnomic way?'

'Oh, I like that!' He nodded approvingly. 'You've really studied the type, haven't you? I suppose you're making a case study of your friends in there,' he nodded towards the house. 'Aren't you going to invite me in?'

'*You?*' She looked at him aghast. 'If I had the slightest idea what you're talking about I'm certain the answer would *still* be no!' She gave a toss of her head and made as if to brush past him, but he put out his hand.

'Whoa there, lady. It's not as easy as that. I told you, we've decided it'd be safer to have you where we can see you.'

'*What?*'

'Say goodbye and thanks, get your things, and let's go.'

'Sorry?'

'Look, sweetheart. Drop the act, OK? It's great. It's really convincing. Full marks. I misjudged you. And I'm real sorry. You've obviously got far more talent than I gave you credit for. I've always seen you as just a pretty face with a rich daddy. You know that. But I'm willing to admit, it was my mistake.' He gave a mock bow with nothing remotely like apology in his eyes and put out a hand to grasp her by the elbow.

'Don't touch me!' She stepped away, regretting the action at once as it put him between her and the safety of the house and goodness knew what he was going to do next.

'Don't *touch*?' He gave a deep chuckle. '*You've* changed your tune somewhat! Still, I don't suppose it goes with the cut-ice English accents. You really go the whole hog, don't you? Miss All-or-nothing!' He gave a bantering smile to signal that his words meant more than they seemed and Emma was once again floundering to make sense of him.

She put a hand over her brow. 'Look,' she said after a brief pause. 'You've obviously got me mixed up with someone else. I'm Emma Andrews——'

'Emma Andrews of Belgravia. Excellent, my dear,' he mocked in another parody of her accent. Without saying anything else he took her by the elbow and started to drag her up the steps towards the door.

'*No!*' What would Lady Burley say if this madman started causing a scene inside? 'Let me go, you damned brute!' she muttered fiercely under her breath. 'You've got the wrong woman!'

'I've been saying that from the very beginning, sweetness. But who would listen with you batting your eyelashes at all and sundry? I stood about as much chance as an ice cube in hell. Even now they're still willing to give you the benefit of the doubt! I had half a mind to keep quiet about running into you yesterday, but I guess something like fair play came into it—not a concept you would understand, of course!'

'What the hell is this?' By now she was beginning to lose her temper. 'You've certainly got half a mind if you imagine I'm going to let you push me about! Who the hell do you think you are? Let me go or I'll scream!' She knew she wouldn't, couldn't, because it would alert someone in the house and then there would be a scene, and then she would lose her job. She wasn't going to lose her job for this patronising brute even if he was the world's most handsome man, damn him. 'I'll count to ten and if you haven't let go I shall——'

'I shall skweam and I shall skweam,' he mocked. Then he dragged her roughly towards him so that his eyes were glowering darkly down into hers with an expression that froze her to the tips of her toes. He lifted his free hand and took hold of her by the jaw, turning her face up to his so that his lips, those still tantalising lips, hovered just above her own, and then they began to move.

'Listen to me, sweetheart, and listen well,' he said huskily. 'I'm taking you back. Whether you like it or not. I'll ask you one last time, do you want to go in and get your things or do you want to come back later for them?'

'I haven't got any things,' she muttered. Then she frowned. 'What things would I have?'

'Sleeping things?' He raised one eyebrow, mocking her again.

'Don't be ridiculous!'

'It was a joke, honey. I know what sleeping things— or lack of them—you prefer. You've told me often enough!' He licked his lips. 'Hell, you'd try the virtue of a saint. When I'm in charge——' He broke off and his eyes narrowed. 'I suppose you're going to say you know what I'll do when I'm in charge?' He quirked another eyebrow.

'Believe me,' she said faintly, 'I haven't a clue what you'll do in the next ten seconds, let alone when you're in charge of whatever it is that's going to have the undoubted benefit of being anything whatsoever to do with you——' She broke off, not sure whether she was making sense even to herself. When his thumb moved silkily over the skin of her cheek like that she was bereft of all ability to think straight. 'Don't,' she muttered, shutting her eyes so she wouldn't have the torment of seeing those irresistible lips so close to her own.

'*Don't*?' He gave a deep-throated chuckle. 'That's the first time I've ever heard you say that. . .when you research you really research. I take my hat off.'

This time he sounded genuinely admiring, despite the heavy measure of irony that laced his words, and Emma opened her eyes to check on his expression. He was gazing at her with a strange, thoughtful look, until the moment he saw her watching him. Then the by now familiar cynical smile came back. 'I do believe there are depths to you I haven't plumbed.' His lips clamped firmly over his perfect teeth.

Despite the shrieks of common sense ringing in her ears, she found herself willing him to bend his head. Kiss me, commanded a silent voice. She took a deep breath and turned her head before the siren song took control.

'You're always putting your arms around me in public. You must be very friendly with whoever it is you think I am. In the circumstances I would have thought you'd have realised your mistake by now,' she said in a rush. 'Or do you never admit to making mistakes?'

Her words had the advantage, or, depending on how you looked at it, the disadvantage, of making him let her go entirely. He stepped back a couple of paces. For a brief second there was uncertainty on his face.

Eager to press home whatever advantage she seemed to have, Emma went on, 'Some people have doubles, and maybe I have, but even you must surely detect *some* difference between us? Even if it's only clothes,' she added as an afterthought.

He gave a short laugh, instantly wiping any sign of

uncertainty from his expression. 'Clothes? Of course, that's the obvious difference. *Too* obvious! It's exactly the sort of point you would focus on. I must say I think I almost prefer this slightly dishevelled, down-at-heel, jumble-sale look. It suits you somehow, especially with your hair flying around all over the place.'

'*What*?' Emma felt her cheeks glow. A brief glance showed her that she was dressed as usual. '*Jumble* sale?' She was wearing a long brown cardigan—all right, so it was from a charity shop—but it was worn over a good tweed skirt she'd had for years, and a perfectly presentable white silk blouse Olga had bought her for her sixteenth birthday. Her shoes were hand-stitched brown leather. After yesterday her high heels were almost ruined. 'Lady Burley seemed to rather approve of my clothes,' she snapped. 'What do you think you know about style anyway?'

'Nothing at all if you're in it,' he came back irritably. 'Can we quit this wrangling and get on? If you're not going in for anything, what's keeping us?'

'I am.' She drew herself up.

'I've had to park the car on the other side of the square,' he explained with exaggerated patience. 'I'm not going to manhandle you all the way across there in full view of a goggle-eyed public. Even though that's probably what you're angling for.' And before she could burst in, he went on, 'I'll ask you one last time. Are you coming quietly?'

'Definitely not. I'm not coming at all!'

He raised both eyebrows and gave her an amused glance which she ignored as being beneath contempt. Then he gave a theatrical sigh. 'Preserve me from spoilt little rich girls. All right. Suit yourself. But I'll spell it out for you so there's no mistake. Show up tomorrow morning. I know it's a day early, but one or two things have come up that have to be discussed. If you're not there——' He paused and gave her a hard, raking glance, which she knew in her bones meant business. 'If you're not there,' he repeated, 'you're out. For good. And you ring your old man and scream blue murder if you like. I mean it. You take the conse-quences yourself. And to hell with you. And him. And the whole set-up if it comes to that!' With a last hard stare he turned as if to walk away.

'*Wait*!' She put out a hand and felt her fingers close with breath-stopping slowness over the smooth leather of his sleeve. He meant what he said. What if it was as serious for the girl he thought he was talking to as it obviously was for him? What would happen if she didn't—as she couldn't—turn up to meet him? What terrible catastrophe would result?

'You've got this all wrong,' she explained in a voice that was suddenly trembling as he swung back to face her. Her fingertips tingled and she felt she could never let go.

'What?' His anger seemed to have drained out of him. Together they stood in the square, linked by that one hand on the arm. Emma felt suddenly dizzy. She couldn't let him go. She didn't understand it, him, any of it. Only one thing was certain. She had to see him again.

'Tell me where to meet you,' she asked breathlessly. 'I'll be there.'

'That's more like it. Come to the centre. Room 303.'

'What——?' She bit her lip. 'What centre?'

'You really push it, baby. You really do. In role to the bitter end? I mean of course the television centre,' he enunciated as if it went against the grain to humour her. 'Nine-thirty prompt.'

'But I can't! Lady Burley——' Then she broke off.

She would square things up in that direction later. She couldn't back out now. Besides, she told herself as he moved away down the side of the square, there was a mystery here, and she would get to the bottom of it.

Her agreement to meet him again, of course, had nothing whatsoever to do with the strange feeling that destiny had picked her up—and was whirling her around in a most unexpected way!

What, she wondered, would Judy and the stars have to say to this?

CHAPTER TWO

JUDY was out all evening so Emma didn't get a chance to consult her, but before leaving Lady Burley's she had already taken the step of having a word with the secretary and was assured that it would be all right if she took the morning off.

The cataloguing was going so well she would have been surprised if she'd been refused, but right up until the last minute she had had a sneaking hope that she would be prevented from keeping her assignation at the television centre.

Now she really had to give the matter some thought, she realised what a crazy situation she was in—she didn't even know the name of the man she was supposed to be meeting!

Defiantly wearing her 'jumble-sale clothes' she took the Tube to Tower Hill and then asked directions. Within a few minutes she was stepping warily through smoked-glass doors into a spacious steel and marble reception hall. A bank of upholstered seats ran down one side beneath a wall of glass that gave on to a palm-filled atrium. Opposite the doors was a reception desk and she headed towards it, not quite sure what she was going to say.

She needn't have worried. Before she was even halfway across the grey marble expanse, a figure detached itself from a group standing near the lifts to her right.

'Cosy!' A plump, dark-haired woman, immaculately

made-up, bore down on her, arms outstretched in welcome.

Emma shot a look over her shoulder, but she wasn't mistaken. The woman was heading straight for her. She felt herself taken up in a motherly embrace, then with a jangling of bracelets the woman began to shepherd her towards the group by the lifts. 'Here she is, the naughty girl! I told you everything would be all right!'

The group, two men and an older woman, began to smile. 'We can split, then, can we?' said one of the men giving Emma an amused glance. 'Brick's sure going to be one happy guy!' He took out a phone from his jacket pocket and punched in a few numbers as he spoke. 'She's down in Reception and coming up fast!' he said into the mouthpiece. 'See ya!' He slipped the phone out of sight. 'See you later, Sybil. Don't be late!'

'Sybil', thought Emma in confusion, shooting a glance at the woman who had dragged her over to the group. Obviously she was in league with the dark stranger of yesterday. He had mentioned a Sybil. But how could he have persuaded these other people to go along with him too?

The other three were already moving off with further goodbyes and sympathetic glances at Emma. She turned when they'd gone. 'Perhaps you'll tell me what's going on?' she asked.

Sybil gave an admiring grimace. 'Brick said you'd been doing your homework. He's certainly impressed. I've never heard him say a good word about your acting till now! Keep it up, sugar. You've made a very smart move!'

'I'm sorry?'

Sybil pressed the call button and the lift doors opened. 'Third floor. He's up there right now. I'll have to run, but I'll see you at the house before I leave tonight. Be good!' With that she pushed Emma into the lift just as some other people got in. The doors closed before she could make a move to get out. She darted forward, a fraction too late, then stepped back, looking at the other occupants and feeling foolish when they avoided her glance. She bit her lip and resigned herself to being whisked upwards to where 'he' was waiting. By 'he', Sybil must mean the stranger. Brick? She frowned. She would certainly have something to say to *him* when they came face to face!

When the doors opened on the third she got out, checking her direction from the room indicator, and made her way as rapidly as she could along the corridor. Several swing-doors later she came to Room 303. There was no name-board on the door to give her a clue about the mysterious Brick. She knocked, just to be polite, then pushed it resolutely open.

He was leaning against the window-sill directly opposite the door as if to be certain of seeing her the minute she stepped over the threshold. There was a telephone receiver in one hand and he had obviously just finished making a call. The line must be red-hot, she was thinking. His eyes were on hers as he replaced the receiver without saying anything.

The impact of seeing him again made her suck in her breath. 'Perhaps,' she began in a rush before she succumbed to his air of authority, 'you'll tell me what this is all about?'

'Thank you for coming over,' he said coolly after a pause. 'I didn't know whether I was being a fool to trust you.'

'I'm entirely trustworthy,' she replied in a voice like ice. 'When I say I'll do something, I do it. Now, will you answer my question?'

'Listen, baby. You've done real well,' he replied in a voice as soft as molten honey. 'I've already told you that.'

'Tell me why I'm here!' she demanded, her own voice rising to counteract the seductiveness of his. She stepped across the room. 'I've done my bit,' she told him fiercely. 'Now do yours!'

She was swept by a sudden anger now she was face to face with him again, and all she wanted to do was hit him until he untangled the strange web he had so unexpectedly woven around her. She was shocked by such a physical reaction to him, but it was his cool, almost supercilious assumption of the right to call the shots that got through to her. Plus the sheer frustration of not knowing what on earth was going on.

'Cool it, will you?' he intoned, still soft-voiced. 'I will not be pushed around. You brought this on yourself. If you didn't regard every man as the pushover your poor old daddy is maybe we'd get somewhere——'

'I haven't got a father!' she exclaimed through clenched teeth.

'All right, so he's not your real father, but you know what I mean. What I'm saying still stands!'

'Naturally. You're the type who thinks everything he says still stands. Even when you're blatantly wrong!'

'At least you're not playing all girly for once. I've always told you you'd be more effective with me if you stood your ground instead of relying on your big blue eyes to get what you want. I'm glad you're learning new methods!'

'Methods? Why should *I* be interested in methods? I don't want anything. Least of all from you. Except——' she corrected herself hurriedly '—the answer to all this nonsense.' She glanced round the impersonal little office they were in. 'Why here?'

'I've been meeting the British film crew. They'll be at the house tonight so you can all get to know each other. Understandably they were worried when you vanished. And with Jon lighting out for Paris with only a day's warning, well——' He jerked his head irritably. 'It's wasting my time to have to come over here, nursemaiding you both. I thought Jon Roe could be trusted at least.'

His eyes were glinting dangerously and she realised he was in a furious rage, but was determined not to lose control. He wore a brooding look and demanded, 'Why the hell do you imagine I came over? If Greg knew how worried we'd all been he'd be right back where he was two months ago—in Intensive Care! If you had an ounce of consideration you'd have thought of that!'

Emma ran a hand through her hair and closed her eyes. Instead of clearing up, everything seemed to be making less sense than ever. 'Please,' she asked in a suddenly confused tone, 'may we take this step by step? Whether you believe me or not I really haven't a clue what you're talking about.'

She moved away from him. He was in autumn shades today, but with the same dark brown leather jacket she had touched yesterday. During the night she had managed to convince herself that the good looks that had swept her off her feet the previous day had been three-quarters imagination. Imagination recollected in tranquillity. Not so, she thought now. He was every bit as devastating as she had first seen!

'I'll get you a cup of coffee,' he said suddenly. 'You look all in. I'd sure like to know what you've been up to!' He shrugged and glanced away. 'I hope you're not sickening for something. That'd really put the kibosh on everything.' He had to pass close to her to reach the

internal phone on the desk beside her. As he leaned
across he gave her a raking glance. 'Are you all right?'

'Of course I'm not all right!' she exclaimed, holding
on to the back of a chair. 'You make me feel as if
I'm——' She fished around for words that would
adequately explain her confusion. 'I feel,' she said at
last, 'as if I've picked up someone else's script. Now if
you'd just tell me which play I'm in, maybe I could
take it from there?' It was a sort of joke. A way of
distancing herself from the odd feelings that were
sweeping over her, but he took it up at once.

'This isn't some film script, Cosy. For once you're
going to have to come down to earth. This is *real life*!
That's why I'm here. You don't imagine I *wanted* to
come over, do you? I've been trying to tell you this!
You can do terrible things to Greg if you're not careful.
It's touch and go whether he'll survive. I care for that
man and I thought you did. Hell, child, you're all he's
got! It's not going to hurt you to quieten down a bit.
Keep your name out of the papers for a few weeks.
Stop rocking the boat. You *owe* it to him, damn it.
And I shouldn't even have to say this to you.'

Emma slid down into a chair. 'My name,' she began
slowly, 'is Emma Andrews. I'm twenty-one. I live in a
bedsitter in——'

'Cosy, *stop it*!' He paused with his hand on the
telephone, sudden fury controlled by a hair's breadth.

When she raised her eyes his own were two hard
black stones outstaring her. She gave an involuntary
shiver. 'I haven't done anything wrong. . .' she managed to say. He made her feel as if she were guilty of
some dreadful crime. 'I can't be guilty when I haven't
done anything wrong,' she told him. She wished he
wouldn't look at her like that. Despite the hostility in

his eyes, there was something else that called out to her. She felt shaken to her soul.

He felt it too. She saw his hand reach out to touch her upturned face. His fingers slid down the side of her cheek, then back to her temples in a slow rhythm that made her heartbeats kick. Her lips seemed to burn with the desire to feel his touch, and she half turned her head, conscious in one sudden dizzying moment of the scent of his skin, the warmth of it, the firmness of his touch.

'I don't even really know your name,' she muttered, reddening as she saw he could read her soul.

'Thank you,' he said huskily and half humorously. 'Nice to know I'm so forgettable.'

'Hardly that. . .' she murmured, unconsciously matching his tone with a lowering of her own voice.

'You would never forget me, would you, baby? After all you've said? After all your promises?' His fingers pressed gently into the roots of her hair at her temple, and then before she knew what was happening his hand slid deep into the long hair, cradling her head and bringing her face closer to his own as he leaned forward. Then his lips were moving over hers, drinking in her sweetness as if surprised to find such pleasure there. Her open mouth gave to him with a stab of pain, a yearning she had never felt before, and a murmur of surprise came from deep in her throat.

Reluctantly he lifted his head and moved back, though his hand still curved round the back of her head. 'And I swore I'd never do that——' He broke off with a wry smile. 'I hope you don't imagine you're going to add me to your scalp-belt, honey.' His hand slid away, lingering in the tangle of long fair hair even as he gave a lop-sided, self-mocking smile and added,

'Do you want your coffee up here in a paper carton or shall we go somewhere a little more——' he smiled ironically '—a little more intimate?'

Emma gripped the side of the desk to steady herself. 'Please explain in words I can understand.'

'Explain what? The way you make me feel?' He raised his eyebrows in a sardonic smile.

'Who do you think I am? You called me Cosy just now. So did the woman downstairs. She must have thought she recognised me too. I don't understand. Is Cosy supposed to be a nickname? Or is it some sort of real name you both decided to choose? Obviously you're in this together. . .'

He frowned and didn't answer straight away. Emma went on, 'Why are we meeting here? You mentioned a film crew. Is this some sort of stunt? Candid camera?' She glanced hurriedly round the bare office. And, she wanted to go on, but dared not, why do you kiss me as if you're my lover? Her limbs were shaking and she was glad she was sitting down.

He moved away and went back to his original perch on the window-sill. 'Cosy van Osterbrook. Daughter of the great Greg van Osterbrook.' He glanced humorously across at her with one eyebrow raised. 'I see you're not wearing my ring?' His eyes fastened on her left hand.

Emma gave a gasp. 'This can't be happening. You make me feel as if I'm going mad! I'm not Cosy van whatever you said. I've never heard of her. Nor have I heard of this Greg character. Nor of you——'

'Brick Dryden, to refresh your memory.'

'There's nothing *wrong* with my memory!'

He slid off the window-sill. 'Listen, let's go to the house. You've got to give up this nonsense sooner or later. Even you'll find it difficult to sustain a role for more than an hour or so at one stretch. Come on.' He took her by the arm and tried to pull her to her feet.

'I'm not going anywhere!' She wrenched back, annoyed when she didn't succeed in breaking his hold. 'I came here in the hope that I'd be able to sort things out, and because I didn't want this girl who you were pretending to take me for to get into trouble. I simply don't believe you when you pretend to think I'm called Cosy. And if I'm supposed to be your fiancée you must be very short-sighted if you've genuinely got us mixed up! Unless she's a mail-order bride, of course!'

'Nothing mail order about you, honey. Though it has crossed my mind we'd both have been better off if we'd thought of that avenue first! Now come on!' Once again he tried to pull her to her feet.

'I'm not going anywhere, Mr Dryden—if that's really your name!' She didn't believe anything he told her just now. 'I'm Emma Andrews. Ask anybody I know!'

His knuckles tightened on her arm, but he stopped trying to force her to get up. 'Are you seriously insisting on this charade?' he demanded fiercely.

'It's no charade. It's the *truth*. Now take your filthy, rotten hands off me!'

His grip tightened further. 'How far do you think you can take it, Cosy? Where do you hope it'll lead?'

Tears of frustration filled her eyes. 'Why won't you believe me, you horrible man? What do I have to do to convince you? I wish I'd never agreed to come here! I thought it would clear everything up instead of making it worse!'

He peered as if fascinated by her reaction. 'Real tears?' One finger feathered across her cheek.

'Of course they're real! I feel so——' She gulped, the strength of her emotion stopping her breath for a moment.

'What do you feel, honey?' His voice had lowered intimately again.

'I feel very, very helpless. I feel confused. I feel *angry*!' she finished, shooting him a look. 'You must think I'm stupid if you think I'm going to go along with this when you won't give me any sort of explanation.'

He studied her face for a protracted moment without saying anything. She could see different emotions moving across it. Confusion. Suspicion. Doubt. Then the by now familiar decisiveness replaced them all and he said, 'OK. You're obviously going to endeavour to play this to the bitter end. Your move, then. *Prove* you're Emma Andrews.'

She gave him a triumphant smile. 'Thank you, Mr Dryden. That's the only comprehensible thing you've said since we met. May I?' She indicated the phone.

He spread a hand. 'Be my guest.'

Pursing her lips, she reached for the receiver. She would ring Judy. She would vouch for her. Then she frowned. Judy would be at work. She was with a computer company in West London. What was it called? Emma searched her memory but it was no use.

'Would you wait until this evening?' she asked, already anticipating the shake of the head that greeted this suggestion.

Her hand still hovered over the phone. Having been back in England only three weeks, she hadn't met any of the other inhabitants of the mansion block except to give them a passing hello. Rent was paid directly into the landlord's account at the bank, so she couldn't even ring the landlord.

She reached for the phone again. There was Lady Burley. Jack. Jack would vouch for her.

She had to rummage in her shoulder-bag for her address book as she hadn't bothered to memorise the phone number. Then she heaved a sigh of relief when she got through. It was Lady Burley's secretary who answered, and it was on the tip of her tongue to ask her to vouch for her when she had a sudden picture of how it would look—as if there were doubts about her honesty.

They had waived references at the interview when she had explained she had been abroad for a year and, despite the priceless collection with which she was working, Lady Burley had fixed her with a gimlet eye and pronounced herself confident she could trust her. 'I wasn't on the magistrate's bench for fifteen years for nothing, my dear,' had been her exact words.

Brick Dryden's eyes were still boring into her, so when she got through she said hurriedly, 'It's Emma, Miss Cookham. I wonder if I could have a quick word with Jack?'

She heard the click as the phone was put through, but before she could stop him Brick Dryden took the receiver from her hand, and when Jack's cheery voice came down the line with a 'Wotcha there, Emma, love,' Brick said rapidly, 'To whom am I speaking?'

She heard a pause, then Jack, more cautiously, went on, 'Lady Burley's butler, sir, can I help?'

'You sure can. Do you happen to know a blonde young woman called Emma Andrews?'

'Yes, sir,' she heard Jack reply at once. 'Has anything happened?'

'I'd like you to tell me how long you've known her. Would it be about three weeks?'

Emma gave a gasp. How did Brick Dryden know that? Jack gave his confirmation. There was a note of puzzlement in his voice, clearly audible down the line.

'Is there any problem, sir?' Emma wondered why he sounded so respectful. He hadn't even clapped eyes on

Brick Dryden. She looked at him now with dislike. He really played the big boss. Poor Jack had recognised that even over the phone!

It was all too easy to detect the note of triumph in Dryden's voice as he thanked Jack for his help. He replaced the receiver.

'Good try, Cosy. But you might have saved yourself the trouble of making that call. It was obvious the truth would come out. So you went there straight away, adopting this fanciful name of Emma Andrews along with an English accent, did you? What was it for? Some sort of research? You really thought you'd prove me wrong about your acting ability, did you?' He chuckled. 'That was a very incautious remark of mine. I'll think twice in future!'

Emma looked at him in bewilderment.

'Don't look so confused, baby. It makes me want to kiss you again,' he said abruptly. 'I certainly prefer you like this. Fighting. Then wide-eyed and innocent. It makes you look real for once. Instead of like a high-gloss pin-up!'

She brushed a hand over her forehead. 'Maybe there's somebody else who's known me a little longer,' she began weakly. 'An old schoolfriend.' She racked her brains, but couldn't think of anyone she could track down straight away. She hadn't kept in touch after school. Everybody had seemed to split up, either to go away to college, or to marry. It was all too easy to lose touch. And then her year vagabonding about the world hadn't helped. 'My passport,' she said suddenly. 'Will that prove what I'm saying?'

He gave her a sardonic glance. 'You don't give up, do you?'

'Look, I don't see why I should be the one to have to prove who I really am. You're the one with the doubts and the accusations. It should be you proving I'm this Cosy whoever she is. But just to make things simple I'm quite willing to go round to the flat and pick up my passport. Would that satisfy you?'

Again there was the sardonic raising of the eyebrows she had noticed yesterday. She blushed.

Fortunately he went on, 'That would, as you say, satisfy me—if you had a passport in the name of Emma Andrews. But,' he added, 'even you couldn't go that far.'

'I'll go and get it.'

He shook his head. 'Tsk, tsk, Cosy dear. Do you forget who you're dealing with? You don't expect me to let you simply walk out of here, do you? You'd vanish within seconds. Wherever you go, I go. I'm going to be with you every step of the way from now on, just until we get this show on the road. Understand?'

Emma shook her long fair hair and gave a sigh. 'Will you come with me, then?' she asked almost humbly. 'It's at the flat.'

'Flat? In Belgravia, you mean?'

She shook her head. 'Nothing so grand. Have you got a car?'

He nodded.

'What are we waiting for?' She made as if to move towards the door, but he caught her by the shoulder.

'If you're wasting my time, or hoping to get away, I warn you, Cosy, you won't do it. My patience has really been tried this morning, and if it weren't for Greg I'd put you over my knee and give you the good hiding you should have had when you were ten!'

'How dare you?' She stepped back.

Brick Dryden gave a deep-throated chuckle. 'You're

quite something, Cosy. I think I'm beginning to understand your famous fascination. Maybe you've just
never bothered to use it on me before. . .'

He lifted a hand and reached out for her, pulling her
unresistingly into his arms. 'Don't count on my dancing
attendance like all the others, but maybe I'll play your
game for a little while. . .' He didn't finish what he was
going to say in words, the kiss he pressed on her lips
being eloquent enough.

Despite herself Emma felt her resistance ebb.
Nothing that had passed between them had contained
one single element of truth—except for this, his touch,
the magic that was conjured into existence when they
were in each other's arms. The moment was over all
too soon.

'Come on.' He was the first to break away. 'Let's get
out of this place. We have to be at the house later
today, but we'll call in at this so-called flat of yours on
the way if you insist.'

Knowing it was fruitless to ask for or offer explanations, she allowed him to push her towards the door
and together they made their way down through
Reception and out to the waiting car without speaking.

What Brick Dryden hadn't told her was that there
was a chauffeur sitting in his car.

'Hi, Cosy. Nice to see y'again,' he greeted her as she
climbed in.

She shot him a startled look, then flicked round to
see what reaction there was from Dryden. He tightened
his lips over a confident smile and got in beside her.

'You can't win 'em all, Cosy, you should have known
that,' he murmured. 'Now, then, are you still determined to call in at this flat of yours? I suppose we can
at least pick up some of your clothes if that's what you

want.' He looked at the ensemble she had on. 'I suppose you'll be back to the glamour-girl look tonight? Impress the film crew?'

Emma closed her eyes and sighed. 'Just keep your thoughts to yourself until you've had a look at my passport,' she told him.

'Where to, then?' He was beginning to look thoroughly bored at what he obviously thought was sheer obstinacy on her part. Her own lips tightened. She would show him. He would have to eat his words. There was a perverse satisfaction in that, even though it would spell the end of the relationship when he realised she wasn't his fiancée.

She told the driver where she lived and settled back, closing her eyes to signify she was as bored by the whole business as he was. The sooner it was all over, the better. She didn't like her emotions being whirled around in this dangerous manner. Life was unpredictable enough as it was without her being made to feel she didn't even know her own name!

In less than twenty minutes she was leading the way up the steps to the front door and letting them both into the gloomy entrance hall. Their footsteps rattled over the lino and he stomped upstairs after her without a word.

When she reached the top floor she unlocked the door to her room and led the way inside. When she turned he was standing in the doorway, a look of sheer astonishment on his face.

'You mean you've actually been living in these conditions?' he exclaimed when his eyes finally came to rest on hers. He moved on swiftly into the room, glancing round, then going over to the one window that had a riveting view over a railway track.

'It's humble, but it's home,' she said stiffly. Inside she was seething. How dared he? Who did he think he was? She knew it was spartan, but it cost as much as she could afford at present and at least it was clean. For a moment she was so blinded by anger she felt like kicking him out. Then she looked at the formidable shoulders, the tall, rangy, muscular bulk of him and knew it would be hopeless. She would have to call the police or something to get him out, and even then he would probably persist in this stupid charade and declare she was an imposter!

Swallowing her feelings, she went over to the bedside table and took out the passport that lay within. 'Satisfied?' she said, flicking it open at the first page and thrusting it into his hands.

He took it warily, even now, she observed, distrust openly visible on his face.

She watched him read it. Then he turned it over, scrutinised the embossed lettering on the front, opened it again and read what was written inside with a growing frown. Then he looked into her face, glanced back at the photograph inside, then shook his head.

'Well, I'll be damned.' He gazed at her for a long time without speaking. The silence went on. He opened the passport again and peered at her photograph.

'If you imagine it's some sort of forgery I suggest you take it to the British Passport Office in Petty France,' she said in a voice like ice. 'And if they don't convince you, perhaps you'll consider the fact that, as you can see from the pages inside, it's been rubber-stamped by the customs authorities of a number of countries. Of course,' she went on sarcastically, 'it may be that they're all wrong. Mr Brick Dryden couldn't be the one who's in the wrong, could he?'

'Come over here.' He grabbed her wrist and pulled

her over to the window, then jerked her face to the light and gave it a thorough scrutiny. 'It's uncanny. If this is the genuine article, you must be sisters. Twins. You're as damn near identical as anything I could imagine.'

Even now she could tell he wasn't completely convinced and he confirmed it by going on, 'It's not some elaborate joke, is it? I mean, I've never looked closely at one of these things before.' He weighed the passport in the palm of his hand. 'Looks authentic——'

'Oh, for heaven's sake! Would anybody go to such elaborate lengths to make a fool out of you, Mr Dryden? I'm pretty sure it wouldn't be too difficult to achieve if that was the name of the game!'

Instead of rising to the bait, he began to chuckle. 'I guess I have to concede. . .for the time being,' he added ominously.

He was still holding her wrist and, instead of letting it drop, he went on holding it, though now it was done not with the intention of restraining her but with a different intention entirely. She felt something change, a sort of increased heat in his blood—his fingers moving in undisguised pleasure as they explored the fold of her wrist.

There was a moment when neither of them spoke— as if they were simultaneously taken over by the sudden electric charge in the air. Emma could feel the tension in him, building and building, and though she didn't understand it she knew she should pull away. But she couldn't. She was helpless to move. It was as if she was being held by far more than his light, fingertip pressure.

When he eventually let her wrist drop he wore a thoughtful expression and he moved away with an abrupt gesture, running one hand rapidly through his short dark hair before muttering half to himself, 'I've

sure fallen for this——' He broke off and gave her a
swift glance, and the stunned look in his eyes vanished
as he took a hold on himself. He frowned. 'OK. . . So
where the hell is Cosy?'

Emma was in a total confusion. His moods changed
so quickly. What had that look meant a few moments
ago? No time to ponder it now. She raised her chin.
'That, I would suggest, is your problem. Now,' she
went on in a shaky voice, 'perhaps you'd do me the
favour of leaving? We've taken up enough of each
other's time and I'm sure we have nothing further to
say to each other.'

'Oh, no, oh, no, honey,' he said at once. 'You've got
it wrong this time at least.' He came back to where she
was still standing with her back to the window.

When he was beside her he looked over her shoulder
across the rail-yards for a long moment, then he tilted
her chin in one hand, his eyes, brilliant with something
as yet unsaid, probing her upturned face. 'This,' he
told her with a thickening of his tone, 'this, my sweet,
mysterious stranger, is only the beginning!'

CHAPTER THREE

'MAY I take a seat?' Brick demanded abruptly.

Emma looked from the leatherette armchair in front of the gas fire to the single bed in the corner. 'I suppose so.' She shrugged, leaving it up to him where he sat.

He followed her glance, gave an amused lift of his eyebrows, and parked himself casually on the arm of the one chair. Emma herself went across the room and sat gingerly on the edge of her bed.

'I'd better tell you a little about myself, especially as I'm probably going to have to ask you one very big favour,' he began. 'I'm Canadian, based in Vancouver,' he told her. 'Various business interests which I won't bore you with, timber, printing, that sort of thing, and more relevantly I've just begun to acquire an independent television company. I say begun,' he frowned, 'because the man I'm buying out is an old family friend, a real autocrat and nothing he ever does is simple. The fact that his only child is Cosy, the girl you so uncannily resemble, has a lot to do with the present confusion.'

He paused and seemed to be choosing his words carefully before continuing. 'Cosy and I became engaged a couple of months back. She's a television presenter. A good one. Nice, light style. Got quite a following back home. But Greg knew I had doubts about whether she would fit in with the new image I want for the company. He's making things difficult because of a misguided sense of concern over Cosy's future and he wants to make sure she's got a say in things when I take over.'

He frowned slightly. 'To make things worse, he had a stroke a few weeks back. Nothing signed. Business on the rocks. His heir, or in this case heiress, Cosy, would lose everything if he died before he signed. In the circumstances it's difficult to hurry things along and he, the stubborn old fool——' He broke off and gave a rueful smile. 'He's playing for time. Thinks I don't know what he's up to. He wants to be quite convinced I'll keep Cosy on the books. He assumes, quite wrongly, she's incapable of looking after herself. But that's a common reaction she gets from men. . .from men of all ages.'

He put his hands in his pockets and looked thoughtful before swivelling to fix her with a bleak smile. 'Cosy and I have had our differences, as you've probably guessed. She came over here three weeks ago——' he shot her a glance '——some coincidence there?'

'That's why you asked Jack how long he'd known me?'

He nodded. 'She came over here to make a documentary with a British crew. It was a sort of test. To see if she could turn out a decent piece of work that didn't rely entirely on the fact that she was Greg van Osterbrook's daughter and had more to offer than her particular brand of spurious Hollywood glamour.'

Emma wondered at the harshness of this judgement, and she felt a fleeting sympathy for the hapless Cosy. But Brick went on.

'I knew she was worried about the assignment. But it never crossed my mind she'd be worried enough to disappear.' He spread his hands. 'You can see why I pounced on you when I saw you. If she doesn't show up, not only will Greg have to be told she's gone to ground, but the whole project will fall through and I'm going to have to do battle with a very sick man. Not something I relish. You understand?'

Emma nodded. She was chilled by his apparent ruthlessness, but could understand his reluctance to keep someone on his payroll—even if it was his fiancée—who couldn't do the job. When their eyes meshed there was a sudden, unexpected flash of sympathy. Instead of acknowledging it, though, Brick rose to his feet and went over to the table where the passport lay. 'I'll have to borrow this for a few hours, of course.'

She stiffened. 'You still don't trust me?'

'You've let me down too often. I mean——' he ran a hand through his hair in momentary confusion '—Cosy's let me down. She can't be trusted. How do I know you're not the same?' He swivelled towards the window and she caught a glimpse of his expression as he turned.

Something about it, and about the way he said he couldn't trust his fiancée, struck a chord with Emma. She knew only too well what it was like to find trust misplaced. It was a feeling familiar from when she had been shunted around from one foster-parent to the next. As soon as she had started to feel she could open out and rely on someone she would be whisked away again.

Now, despite the lesson she had learned in the past, she had already begun to open up to Brick Dryden, and she knew she would pay the penalty if she didn't close up again—and pretty quickly too. Yet she thought she understood how he must be feeling. It pulled her two ways because she knew it would be madness to allow her sympathies to be aroused any further.

With an effort she managed to freeze off her naturally understanding response and say coldly, 'You don't imagine I care a damn whether you trust me or not, I hope. But I can't help feeling rather insulted by your attitude. I didn't *have* to bring you back here to prove I was telling the truth. And to find that even that doesn't convince you is insupportable. Who do you think you are to doubt my word?'

He had reached out for her passport as she began to speak, and she gave him a long, cool stare, her heart-shaped face, framed by its wild tangle of fair hair, expressing her complete disdain for him.

He hesitated with his fingers curling round the edges of the passport, and when he picked it up he held it challengingly in his hand and said, 'If you have nothing to hide you won't mind if I check it out, surely? You're not planning on using it in the next couple of hours, I take it?'

'That's not the point. It's my property. I don't know you from Adam. Just because you arrange to meet me in some flashy television centre you seem to imagine that supplies you with suitable credentials. You could be anybody for all I know—an international gangster, anything!'

She rose to her feet and moved towards him with her hand outstretched, expecting him to relinquish the passport.

They stood facing each other, challenge written equally on both their faces. She could see he was waiting for her to give in, but she stood her ground. '*Well*?' She waited. When he didn't react straight away she went on, 'And while we're about it, where's *your* passport, Mr Dryden, assuming that really is your name and not some alias?'

Slowly he began to draw his lips back in a mirthless smile. 'Quite right, sweetheart,' he approved. 'Very wise to check me out. My passport is at the house. You're very welcome to have a look at it any time.'

'Yes?' She gave a slight lift of disbelief to her finely arched brows.

'Yes indeed,' he murmured. 'And as I have a meeting down there later on, perhaps you'd like to do it right away?'

'I certainly would.'

'Fair exchange,' he murmured, pocketing her own.

She moved past him with a toss of her head, picking up her leather shoulder-bag and a wool scarf. Let him hang on to her passport for a few minutes if it made him happy! She didn't care. But she would definitely take up his challenge to check *him* out. Why not? She would show him she wasn't to be trifled with. What a nerve he had, probing into her life like this. She would probe back!

'Emma Frost,' he said as they walked across the pavement a few minutes later towards the waiting car. He repeated the name, but she avoided his glance and got in without deigning to reply.

'To the house, Burt,' he ordered through the partition. 'Make it snappy.'

It was only when they were speeding on to the Hammersmith flyover a few minutes later and starting to follow the signs pointing west that Emma brought herself to say something. Her expression was full of alarm. 'Just where are we going?' She turned to him, searching his face as if she could read the answer on it.

'To the house, as I told you,' he replied unhelpfully. 'Isn't that what you want?'

She frowned. 'But where *is* this house?'

'Only an hour down the road.'

'An *hour*?'

He nodded comfortably.

'I asked *where*, not how long you think we're going to be stuck in the traffic.'

'Near Salisbury. Not far.'

'Not *far*?' she gasped. 'I can't go all that way!'

'You people! I know this is a small place, but you sure make it even smaller!'

'Why? What do you mean?'

He shrugged. 'An hour's drive? It's neither here nor there. We've got the road. We've got the vehicle. And we've got the time. So what's the hassle?'

'But it's over a hundred miles!' she exclaimed.

'So?'

She sank back. Really, she thought, she had brought it on herself. She should have checked more thoroughly first. But this was what she was always doing—acting first, thinking afterwards. It had already landed her in hot water. 'I feel as if I'm being kidnapped,' she bit out.

'Very willingly, if I may say so.'

'Thanks. I knew I could expect sympathy and understanding from you.' She scowled and turned to look out of the window at the blur of houses lining the road. Soon they reached more open countryside. They weren't speaking to each other again. He was making notes and dialling on his phone. Trying to impress me, she thought irritably. Big business tycoon. She felt as if she had a perpetual frown on her face. It wasn't as if she wanted to see his damned passport. She only hoped he would have the decency to send her back to town in the car as soon as she'd glanced at it. She didn't doubt it would confirm the name Brick Dryden—whatever that was supposed to prove. By train the journey back would take twice as long.

* * *

When the car slowed it was fifty-five minutes later, and by the time they whispered up a sweeping tarmac drive between banked rhododendrons not yet in bloom it was one hour precisely.

She saw him glance at his watch and give her a swift, satisfied smile. She ignored it and followed him out of the car up a flight of shallow steps to the portico of a large, white, Queen Anne mansion.

'Very pretty,' she couldn't help murmuring. 'Do you own or lease?'

He shot her a narrowed glance as if to tell her to mind her own business.

'Just checking you out,' she returned.

'Own it,' he replied swiftly, with a short laugh. 'But not personally.'

Wondering what he meant by that, she waited until he let them both inside. The chauffeur had already floated the limousine round the side of the house.

'The guys are probably here already,' he informed her. 'Is it back to Cosy or are you still playing Emma Frost?'

'Emma Andrews,' she retorted.

'Emma Andrews Frost. We'll have to see what we can do to thaw you out.' Before she could come back with the cutting riposte that sprang to mind he was heading across the hall to a door on the far side. 'Come along,' he beckoned. 'We will have that coffee we discussed in town. Go in and make yourself at home.'

Marvelling at the last remark, she made her way into a pleasant, flower-filled sitting-room into which her own bedsitter would fit at least twice over. It was furnished entirely in keeping with the period of the house and she couldn't help admiring whoever had had a hand in its décor before she irritably reminded herself that with Brick Dryden's apparent wealth he would no

doubt call in professional interior designers and give
them *carte blanche*. The thought made her roam criti-
cally to and fro until he came back.

'It won't be a minute.'

'Are you going to get this passport now and let me
go?' she challenged.

'Do you have to be back in town right away?'

She eyed him suspiciously. 'What's that got to do
with you?'

He didn't reply at once, but went to straddle one of
the elegant, straight-backed, eighteenth-century chairs.
Her shock must have registered because he stood up
again and came across to her. Large though the room
was, he seemed too big for it and he prowled round
her like a caged animal viewing its dinner before
leaning up against the marble fireplace and giving her
a quizzical glance.

'Life is never simple,' he informed her superfluously.
'Who would expect somebody like you to be conjured
out of the blue?' Then he said, 'I told you I was going
to ask you to do me one very big favour. And this is
it.'

Just then the door opened and a middle-aged woman
in a flowered overall bustled in with a trolley on which
was an array of titbits to tempt anyone's appetite.
There was a large silver coffee percolator and, noted
Emma, one cup and one saucer and one plate.

'There you are, Mr Dryden. The girl's already taken
the coffee in for you men.'

'Thank you, Miriam. I'll be along in a moment.
Maybe you'd fetch Miss Andrews some magazines or
something for later on. I shall be engaged for about an
hour,' he told Emma, forestalling the angry protestations that were already leaping to her lips.

When they were alone again he spread his hands in

the nearest thing to an apology she guessed he had ever made. 'I told you I had a meeting,' he countered before she had a chance to say anything.

Astounded, she could only gaze at him open-mouthed, but before he could go on and make matters worse she burst out, 'You really take the prize for arrogance, Mr Brick Dryden. First you lure me out into the depths of the countryside—no question of whether I have commitments of my own in town! Oh, no! You whisk me out here without a by your leave! Then, not content with that, you have the gall to assume I'm going to sit twiddling my thumbs here for the next hour, leafing——' she said with scornful emphasis '—through a bunch of magazines! Well, thank you, thank you very much indeed!'

She made angrily towards the door before she remembered something else. 'And oh, yes!' She swung back. 'You were also building up to asking me a favour—on top of all that!'

He looked impatiently at his watch. 'It's too late to start complaining now. You wanted to come out here. You were the one who agreed. I didn't try to persuade you. Now you're here I'm trying to make it as comfortable as possible. Hell, it's a darn sight more comfortable than sitting in that grim little room of yours, isn't it? *And*,' he went on, cutting off her furious outburst, 'I don't see you have any choice in the matter, so wasting time arguing isn't going to get us anywhere. Is it?'

He moved rapidly towards the door, drawing level with her when he reached it. 'You'll just have to learn to make the best of a bad job. I'll see you in one hour!'

He put his hand on the doorknob and had already turned it when she sprang forward, brushing against him with the intention of making her escape, but he caught her by the forearm and pulled her back.

'It's no good your rushing out like that. You've no way of getting back to town from here unless you're prepared to hitch a lift on the main road four miles away, and I'm damn sure I'm not going to allow that. Just calm down. When we've had a chance to talk you'll see things in a different light.' He glanced hurriedly at his watch again.

She took her chance and reached across him to yank open the door, but he hauled her back, one hand running rapidly down the length of her spine in a movement that had nothing to do with restraining her. It was more like an invitation to unrestraint, she registered, averting her head as his lips seemed to shut out all reason by their sudden proximity.

'Let me go!' she managed to gasp before they came down swiftly and confidently over her own.

'Cosy——' he murmured, then checked himself. 'I mean—Miss Frost, you beautiful stranger, whoever you are. . .' His face was no more than an inch from her own.

He held her pressed against his broad chest for one eternal moment so that she was aware of his heartbeats thumping in a wild cacophony with her own. He smelt of leather and soap and wide open spaces. But he belonged to someone else and she wrenched away with a cry of anger.

'Don't. . . It's not right—I—I don't want you to do that,' she lied.

He brought his two hands down on either side of her face, holding it tilted towards his own, so that his dark eyes, sparking with vitality, seemed to stab her all over with points of flame. 'If you're half as confused as I am you're going to need at least an hour to take stock. Be here when I get back. I'd like that, Emma. But it's up to you.'

She felt faint with longing for his kiss again, but tried to distance herself from the turmoil his touch aroused. 'You'd make a very good politician, Brick Dryden, switching on the charm at the drop of a hat,' she breathed, her eyes holding his, a vestige of a challenge remaining in their blue depths.

'Be here,' he murmured, making it sound like a request instead of the command it was.

'I'll stay. If only because I——' she gulped in air from a breath held too long '——if only because I'm fascinated to know what tale you're going to spin me next.'

He laughed softly and his eyes crinkled at the corners, hiding the steel-edged authority which they habitually held. 'Cosy's the one for tall tales. I wouldn't be at all surprised you don't take after her in that respect as well!'

With a brief, plundering kiss full on her trembling lips he released her and pivoted to the door. 'One hour. I promise.'

With that he was gone, and Emma made her way blindly to one of the chesterfields and sank down into its welcoming cushions. Her knees were shaking and she could only stare unseeingly at the carpet until her composure returned. Then there was just one question in her head: when he kissed her, was he kissing *her*, or her look-alike, Cosy van Osterbrook—his fiancée?

To say that an hour would suffice in order to take stock was optimistic. Emma picked at the food provided for her, drank several cups of strong, black coffee, and leafed through one or two magazines the housekeeper had brought in for her. But it was all as nothing. The only reality was the memory of Brick Dryden's touch— and the impossible situation she was in. And what, she asked herself for the hundredth time, was the favour he wished to ask of her? Should she answer with an emphatic negative—no matter what it was? Or should she weigh the pros and cons as, in any other circumstances, she would be wont to do?

Sighing, she got up from the table, flicking an impatient glance towards the carriage clock on the mantelpiece, and went to stand in front of the window. Had it been only the day before yesterday that she had looked out of a window similar to this one and weighed the risks of making a dash through the rain to buy a birthday card? How could life change so drastically in less than forty-eight hours?

Judy's prophecy came back to her, together with her own protestations that she was entirely content with her luck the way it was. Now she had a niggling suspicion that she would never be content again—not having known for however brief a moment the paradise of being in a certain man's arms. It was illogical and went against all her previous experience.

I'm in love, she registered, curious and frightened at the night-to-day change that had taken her unawares. But there was no future in such thoughts. He belonged to someone else. She, Emma Andrews, no matter how closely she was supposed to resemble this other woman, was the outsider, and she had better remember it for her own peace of mind.

She lifted her head as the clock chimed sweetly behind her, and then she turned right round as the door opened and the man who had occupied her thoughts so painfully for the last hour strode briskly into the room.

He came to an abrupt halt when he caught sight of her.

'I'm still here,' she announced, correctly interpreting the lifting of his eyebrows.

He gave a brief nod. 'Any coffee in that pot or is it stone-cold by now?'

He flung himself down on the chesterfield and ran a hand through his dark hair in a gesture that was becoming endearingly familiar.

She came over and lifted the lid of the pot. 'Still hot. But you'll need a cup and saucer.'

'Press that bell beside you, sweetheart. Is there anything Miriam can get you when she comes up?'

Emma shook her head, burningly aware of the word 'sweetheart' and wondering if it was the word of endearment he used when addressing Cosy. 'The only thing I want, Mr Dryden, is answers. You said you had a favour to ask.'

'Yes.' He seemed to have discarded elaborate explanations and plunged straight in. 'I want you to stay over for a few hours. If you have to be back tonight I'll get Burt to drive you home. Otherwise you can stay here. Plenty of room. What do you say?'

'Why do you want me to stay?' She frowned.

'Simple. Cosy still hasn't checked in. The film crew are getting mutinous. And you can play the part better than any other person alive.'

'You mean you want me to impersonate your fiancée?' She sank down on to a chair.

'Look, I know you'll have a hundred objections, but what it boils down to is being yourself but allowing everyone to call you by another name. It's not much to ask. If you're having to have time off work I'll make it up to you. I'll double, treble, the salary you're losing. That's fair, isn't it?'

Emma inspected her fingernails, not trusting herself to match his glance with one of her own. 'You seem to have the knack of making things sound reasonable even when they're not.'

'This is reasonable. What could possibly be unreasonable about it? I'm not asking you to do anything illegal. Those lads won't know the difference. It's just that they've been booked for three weeks starting the day after tomorrow. They need to feel everything's going to go through smoothly. Damn it,' he added testily, 'I don't know what sort of set-up I've taken on—even the director's living it up in Paris. But there's nothing I can do about that. It was our own fault for sending him out ahead of the back-up team. Sybil,' he explained, 'came on a few days later, by which time there was a message waiting at the hotel saying he'd got sick of hanging around and thought he might as well see a bit of Europe.' He scowled. 'Europe seems to mean a no doubt questionable hotel in the Latin Quarter, but that's Montrealers for you.'

'Is it?' She raised her head and gave him a watery smile. 'What if they ask me about the film? What I know about film-making can be written on one tiny corner of a postage stamp.'

'You mean you'll stay? No strings? No hassle? You'll unequivocally stay?'

He looked so astonished and relieved she couldn't help laughing despite the knowledge that she was only digging a deeper pit of despair for herself when the time came to say goodbye, but she nodded. 'I'll stay. Just for this evening. And if Burt will drive me back, that'll be fine.'

'You're a real sweetheart,' he said warmly, sitting up with all sign of exhaustion having vanished in a trice. 'I'll make it very worth your while.'

Privately she doubted that. There was only one thing

that would make the heartache worthwhile and she knew that was out of the question.

She brushed a hand across her face as if to wipe away the web of thought that threatened to spoil the new mood that had sprung up, and said brightly, 'Hadn't you better tell me a little bit more about— well, about the role I have to play? About—about her?'

He reached across for a phone on the low table separating them and dialled a couple of numbers so that Emma guessed it was an internal line. 'Cash, bring me Cosy's biog, will you? I'm in the drawing-room.' He replaced the receiver. 'You've got a couple of hours yet. Time enough to scan her achievements to date. Basically all you have to remember are a few names of the celebs she's interviewed.'

'Celebs?' She arched her eyebrows.

'Movie stars mostly. People everybody knows, so no problem there. Plus a couple of ice-hockey players nobody this side of the water has ever heard of.'

'I wouldn't count on it,' she murmured. 'It'd be Murphy's law to discover the cameraman is an ice-hockey buff. We do have teams over here, you know.'

'You do?' He leaned forward interestedly, then remembering there were more important issues at stake just now he got up and went to the door. 'I'll be right back. I think you'll be surprised by this!'

Emma wasn't left long to puzzle over his words. He returned in a moment with a silver-framed photograph. At first she thought it was herself with a different hairstyle, then she gasped. 'Cosy?'

He nodded. 'Now you know what this is all about.' He gave her a considering look. 'When the show's on the road we're going to get to the bottom of this. It's too weird to be due to mere accident.' He suddenly sat down beside her. 'I am sorry, honey. I've piled all this on you and scarcely asked you a single question about yourself. It's not through lack of interest, but lack of time.' He reached out and covered one of her hands with his own. 'You're a real sweetheart. As I said before, this is just the beginning, isn't it?'

'Is it?' she asked. Silently her heart added another question. Is it just the beginning—or is it the end?

CHAPTER FOUR

WHILE Emma skimmed the contents of the folder she was handed, part of her mind was busy with the ramifications of what she had agreed to do. Just now Cash, one of Brick Dryden's assistants, had given her a friendly though somewhat puzzled smile, saying, 'Checking we've got your details right, Cosy?'

And before she could make any sort of answer, discreet or otherwise, Brick had moved smoothly in with, 'She's just being professional, Cash. I'll join you later.' It was a clear indication he wished him to leave.

When the door closed Emma raised her head and fixed Brick with a baleful stare. 'This isn't going to work. You didn't tell me I was expected to fool people who actually know your fiancée——'

'Don't be ridiculous,' he snapped. Obviously she had overstepped the mark in some way. He went on. 'Cash won't be dining with us this evening. I'm not trying to force you to do anything beyond your capabilities. Any fool can hold their own over a simple meal, can't they?'

Emma flinched. 'It's immaterial, isn't it? Why should it matter a damn to me anyway?' she asked him coldly. 'If they guess, that's your problem.'

Brick came right over to her. She could feel the sudden spurting anger like a physical force as he glowered down at her. Then just as suddenly it was replaced by a smile of infinite charm. 'Dear Emma,' he murmured in a voice like velvet, 'have you any idea now much I'm relying on you tonight? I have to go back to Vancouver very shortly. Already people are screaming down the phone for me. But I can't let Cosy make a mess of things. It would kill Greg. And I mean that quite sincerely.'

He slid down on to the chesterfield beside her and she was paralysed by the touch of his thigh against her own. She would have edged to a safer distance but there was nowhere to go. Instead she crossed her legs, lessening the contact, but still aware of every in and out of his breath as he leaned to look over her shoulder at the notes on her lap.

'I know it's confusing for you,' he continued silkily just above her right ear, 'but I'm a generous man. I don't expect you to help me out of a hole without recompense.'

She felt his arm stretch across the back of the sofa.

'Tell me,' he was going on, 'is there any way I can square things with your employer for whisking you away at such short notice today?'

Emma prickled with annoyance. It wasn't just that he was practically breathing down her neck, giddying her senses by the almost seductive attempt to placate her, it was the assumption he could wave a wand and everything would fall the way he planned. That, she told herself, was what really irked her.

'I'm not used to jumping to the crack of a whip, Mr Dryden. You must forgive me if I don't leap to do your bidding with as much alacrity as you wish. . .'

She made a half-turn of her head. He was smiling, not even registering her resentment, but for a brief moment she was aware of nothing else but the dancing, flecked brown-gold lights in his eyes. Slowly her glance sank, first to his nose, then to his mouth and, as if on cue, the lips she had already known parted slightly, teasing her with false promise, taking her in, possessing her, sending her spinning helplessly into the stratosphere.

Time seemed to miss a beat.

The arm that had casually come round across the back of the sofa slipped as if accidentally so that it was circling her waist. She felt it tighten. Now she was wrapped in a heady, expensive aroma of very masculine cologne—but so subtle as to be a mere hint, and for that reason all the more dizzyingly intimate. His head was only inches from her own by now. If she turned, she warned herself, their lips would collide. . . He would be kissing her before she knew what was happening. And she knew why. It was because he wanted a favour from her.

She gave him a cutting glance and, pretending she hadn't noticed the arm encircling her waist, pushed both hands over her hair as if to tidy it.

Before anything else could happen he got up with a muffled exclamation and went to stand across the room beside the fireplace. He avoided her glance and then in a rapid, suddenly rather impersonal voice, began to instruct her on what to expect that evening.

'You have nothing to worry about,' he reaffirmed. 'No one has met Cosy. They've only seen her on screen. Let me do the talking. It should be plain sailing. Now, if you'd like me to call Miriam, she can show you to your room. I imagine you'd like to freshen up. And Emma—please don't bite my head off, but if you'd like to dress for dinner as we usually do, you'll find plenty of clothes up there. Please, make use of them. Most girls like dressing up,' he added as if that disposed of any objections she might have.

'Won't Miriam expect me to know where my room is?' she suggested without expression.

He grimaced. 'I'd better stop calling you Emma too.

Come on. I'll show you up myself then I'll have to leave you for a while.'

Still carrying the folder, she reluctantly followed him out. He led her up a wide flight of stairs with a gallery overlooking the entrance hall, and at the end of a corridor they went up a further flight of stairs to what were evidently residential quarters. He came to a halt outside a white door. 'I'd better have a look to see if you've got everything you need.'

Pushing it open, he led the way inside. It had obviously been occupied fairly recently, though there were signs that the maids had imposed some sort of order. Even so a stack of suitcases with various garments protruding from them stood beside the large double bed. Emma eyed that with a sickening feeling.

'I take it this is Cosy's room?' She lifted her eyebrows, expecting him to add that it was a room they shared, but he merely nodded.

'Use her stuff. She probably went off with only one bag and has forgotten she has any of this.' He was looking down at the suitcases and lifted the lid of one of them.

'I can't wear anybody else's clothes,' Emma began, automatically going over to stand beside him. 'It wouldn't seem right.'

'You intend to come down to dinner in your——' He paused.

'In my jumble-sale clothes, yes.'

He gave a distant smile. 'Maybe you'll have second thoughts when you've had a look round.' He flung open a wardrobe and rifled among the dresses already hanging inside. 'Here, this would suit you. And it hasn't been worn because I bought it for her and——' He paused again.

'And what?' asked Emma shortly, unable to stop

herself from peering over his shoulder at the dress he was holding out to her.

'And she said she'd only wear it for me,' he finished curtly. He swivelled.

'In that case, it's exactly the one I shouldn't wear— if it has associations like that for you both.'

His broad shoulders tensed, and when he turned to her he gave her a slow up-and-down look, a lop-sided smile playing over his features. 'Very sensitive, Miss Frost. Quite unexpected coming from lips from which familiarly I'm used to hearing other sentiments.'

She wondered if it was a comment on her difference from his fiancée. If it was it was like another instance of how hard he was on Cosy. Obviously her disappearance had stabbed his pride. Emma didn't see him as a man who forgave easily. But she herself had no intention of getting involved in his relationship with someone else. It was up to him to work that one out. She moved away. 'What am I supposed to do from now until dinner? More homework?' She indicated the file she carried.

He was brisk again. 'I'm not the best host today. There's too much on my mind. I'm real sorry I have to keep leaving you by yourself. If you feel like it you could have a dip in the pool.'

'Pool?' she gulped.

'Don't worry. It's heated and under cover. I insisted on that in this climate! Come on,' he turned to the door, 'I'll show you how to get down.'

'I haven't got a swim-suit,' she protested mildly as she followed him.

He gave her an amused glance. 'I can assure you, all the staff are being worked off their feet right now. Nobody, but nobody is thinking of swimming—you'll have it entirely to yourself!' He glanced at his watch.

'Let's be quick. The guys are meeting Sybil. It's good that she saw you. Now she can report back to Greg without alarming him.'

'You mean because she thinks she met Cosy this morning?'

He nodded.

'But she didn't.' She was having difficulty in keeping up with him as he was tearing along the lower corridor, taking it for granted she was following meekly in his wake. She felt like stopping right there and digging in her heels, but didn't want to miss his response.

They had reached a pair of double doors when she caught up with him. She saw how set his face was, the expression grim and a warning if ever there was one that she should drop the matter straight away. But she couldn't believe he was as indifferent to Cosy's where-abouts as he seemed to pretend. 'What if she's ill, or been kidnapped, or lost her memory?' she persisted. 'Finding me isn't a substitute, is it?'

'She left a message.' His manner was abrupt. 'It was clear enough she intended to take time out.'

'But,' she persisted, 'it can't have been so detailed, otherwise you wouldn't have made the mistake of thinking she was me hanging around in that bookshop in London. You said at the time how surprised——'

'Drop it, will you?' His black eyebrows drew together, emphasising his murderous expression.

Undeterred, she went on, 'You're asking a lot from me, Mr Dryden, and it makes me feel responsible for her in a way—can't you understand that?'

'Do you imagine I'm not doing every single possible thing in my power to find out where she is?' he intoned in a fierce monotone. 'Do you imagine I'm just sitting back, letting it ride?' His face had darkened and he glowered down at her. 'Well?' he said furiously. 'Do you?'

Emma stepped back, biting her lip. But then she raised her chin. 'I'm sure you're playing your cards close to your chest. I would imagine that's second nature to you, so forgive me for daring to raise a voice in criticism, Mr Dryden. But you haven't shown much evidence of concern so far. Your chief goal seems to be to pacify as many people as possible. With scant regard for the truth.'

He was scowling now, and again his anger rose up like a palpable physical force. She flinched, waiting for its full blast, but instead he thrust open the doors and barged through without adding to what he had already said. She caught a glimpse of glass and palms over his head, then he held the door and she stepped after him.

It was like a tropical paradise inside. There was a flower-filled island in the middle of a pool with a small bar and vibrantly coloured parrots and parakeets swooping among the trailing vines that hung from the glass roof. Rattan chairs were arranged around the edge, and a further door flanked by potted shrubs had a sign, 'Sauna'. Brick looked round as if checking for faults.

'There it is,' he told her with inappropriate savagery in his tone. 'Make use of it if you wish. But please don't feel I'm merely trying to pacify you, will you?' he asked in a voice dripping with sarcasm.

With a dark backward glance he walked the curving side of the pool and poked his head into the sauna. 'It'll take a few minutes to warm up,' he called over his shoulder, adding, 'I'll have someone bring you fresh towels. You have a couple of hours in which to kick your heels before your greatest performance. In the meantime, enjoy everything Rosedene Manor has to offer, won't you?'

By now she was standing beside him, and when he turned to look down at her he added under his breath, 'Everything? Why not?' There was no mistaking the nature of his suggestion, with that double-edged undertone. As if to confirm it he skimmed her body from shoulder to waist with one hand, and then let it linger there for a moment until, just before she protested, he let it drop with an ironic shrug.

'I'm in your debt. You don't have to make it more difficult than it already is,' he said enigmatically. With a closed look on his face he began to move away down the side of the pool. 'I have calls to make to Hong Kong. Can't be helped. See you at dinner. And Emma——' He paused with his hand on the door and, as if it cost him a great effort, he jerked his head once and then, apparently thinking better of what it was he had been about to say, he was gone.

I do not know what to make of him, thought Emma. Of this. Of everything. She was lying in the sauna after her swim, trying to relax but finding it impossible with the turmoil of speculation hammering away at her. In a few hours she would be back in London, back to reality, back to the simple certainties of her daily life. Except that things would be changed now, never to be the same no matter how hard she tried. She would never forget the promise in Brick's smile in those rare moments when there was no challenge and counter-challenge in their exchanges.

She had a final shower and dried herself briskly on one of the towels the maid had brought, and then slipped thoughtfully into a pink bathrobe that had been brought down too. Was it true? she wondered. Was there some connection between herself and Cosy? It was a fact they looked uncannily alike. But what could it mean?

Making her way upstairs to her borrowed room, she half hoped to come face to face with Brick. Time was short. There seemed so much to find out, so much to share, she thought with a small grimace. But that was forbidden territory. Hopes in that direction had to be squashed before they were born.

A gong summoned her to dinner. Brick was already waiting in the hall, and turned to look up as she made her appearance in the gallery. Even at this distance she could feel the electricity crackle through the air between them. She knew why she was so nerve-tinglingly aware of it. For him, she reminded herself, it was simply because she resembled the woman he loved.

Looking more self-possessed than she felt, she glided down the stairs to join him.

'I told you it would suit you,' he murmured as she drew close. 'Keep it. Let it be a gift.'

'But what will Cosy think?' She glanced down at the silk dress she wore.

'Cosy has more clothes than she can wear in a year. She won't even know it's gone.'

Emma thought it unlikely that the other girl would be so indifferent to such a gorgeous gift from the man she was going to marry, but she didn't say anything for Brick was already leading her towards the sitting-room.

He introduced her to the three men who were gathered rather self-consciously in the opulent surroundings of a garden-room where aperitifs were being served, and said, 'They'll be dogging your footsteps for the next three weeks, Cosy, so I suggest we have a complete embargo on shop talk, just for one evening. You can swop yarns to your heart's content next week.'

With their wives and girlfriends present too it was as
easy for Emma to sail through the evening as Brick had
predicted—all she had to do was keep her end of the
light-hearted conversation going. The fact that the
soundman had visited Toronto for a few days was no
problem as Emma had been there herself on her year's
travelling, and she knew she sounded authentic enough
apart from the question of her accent.

When one of the men mentioned it, teasing her for
sounding so English, she surprised herself by quipping,
'When in Rome, as they say.' And, with a hint of a
drawl, she added, 'Brick likes me anglicised, don't you,
honey?' Her eyes, bright with challenge, sought his.
His reaction was to reach over and stroke the back of
her hand where it lay on the table.

'That's right, sweetheart. Go as far as you like. . .'
His own eyes were dancing with malicious amusement
when he detected the beginning of a blush, and she
knew she hadn't imagined the suggestive undertones in
his voice.

It was all soon over. Emma assumed she would be
driving back to town with everyone else until she
realised they were all staying overnight. She felt guilty
at having to drag the chauffeur out at this time of night,
but there was no alternative and she went back upstairs
in order to change back into her own clothes while the
others had a night-cap.

Reluctantly hanging the turquoise silk dress back in
the wardrobe, she knew she couldn't take what
belonged to someone else. Wondering if the housekeeper would remember to have it cleaned, she gave a
sudden start when there was a knock at her door and it
began to swing open. Caught on the opposite side of
the room from where her own outer garments lay, she

was clad only in bra and pants when Brick himself calmly walked in.

'Do you really have to go back tonight?' he demanded irritably, scarcely taking in that she was half undressed.

'How dare you come barging into my room? Will you get out?' she exclaimed before she could stop herself.

He did a double take. 'I've seen you naked often enough!' he gritted.

'I beg your pardon. You've never seen *me* naked!'

'It's the same thing——Oh, I'm sorry.' He ran both hands through his short hair. 'It's been a trying sort of day. I *am* sorry, Emma.' He came further into the room despite her words. 'I keep forgetting you're not Cosy.' Then he lifted his head and gave her that smile that made her heart stop. 'Can you imagine what it's like for me?' he demanded softly. 'I keep wanting to treat you as familiarly as I treat Cosy. It's only when you slap me down I realise I've overstepped the mark. I keep forgetting that for you it's all new.'

'You don't have to remind me,' she said, stifling the knot of emotion that rose to her throat.

'What do you mean?' He came closer and gazed into her face, apparently detecting the tension there for he leaned forward, putting out a hand and gently pushing her hair from her face. 'Are you all right?'

'Of course,' she said through tight lips. 'I did quite well this evening, didn't I? Now I'm going home. The end of the show.'

'No,' he countered. 'Not the end. Not yet. Never the end. . .' He allowed the fingers of his right hand to trail slowly down the side of her face, following the curve of her chin, then, almost as if he was in a daze, he let them slide behind her ear and down the long line of her neck towards her collarbone. His touch seemed to have stunned her and she could only stare wide-eyed in anticipation of what he might do next. The hazel eyes were bright with unmistakable emotion. But what did it mean? It looked almost like love. But he was such an actor.

She saw him draw a breath, mouth opening slightly as if preparing to taste something succulent, then with a catch in his throat he murmured, 'You can't go yet. I don't want you to leave. . .' He seemed to search for a reason and added rapidly, 'Not until all the questions have been answered. . .'

'What questions?' she managed to croak, trying to appear impervious to the way he was looking at her.

'There must be a reason for your similiarity.' He managed to bring a lop-sided smile to his face. 'Look, honey,' he went on as if trying to bring a more reasonable note into his voice, 'I've hardly had the chance to say three words to you since you got here—and now you're leaving.' He hesitated. 'Stay. Let's talk,' he added, his voice thickening. 'I really want you to. . .'

'I *can't* stay. You promised to get me back to London. And besides, I have work to do in the morning.'

'What work, Emma? What is this work you do?' he insisted, fingers beginning to move over the silk of her shoulders.

'I'm cataloguing Lady Burley's family library,' she told him, breathlessly aware of his touch but unable to move away. 'It hasn't been done for about fifty years,' she added, speaking like an automaton. 'Even then it wasn't done properly.'

'If it's waited fifty years, won't it wait another day?'

'I can't keep having time off. What will she think?'

'I'll ring her and find out.'

'No!' She put out a hand to restrain him. He caught it and crumpled it tightly in his own.

'I'll sort things out for you. I've already told you I'll treble the salary she's paying you.' He was squeezing her fingers over and over as if determined to keep her beside him by sheer force.

'It's not the money, Brick, it's—I don't like letting people down. It's not fair.'

He began to laugh, his eyes bright flames of amusement. 'You are wonderful. The honest Miss Frost!' His fingers tightened possessively on her shoulder, pulling her towards him.

'Don't call me that!' she exclaimed, feeling her knees begin to tremble as he showed no apparent sign of releasing her, but instead seemed intent on hauling her into even closer intimacy.

His glance slid over her flushed face with a velvety look she hadn't seen before. 'I seem to remember I promised to thaw you out,' he murmured, pulling her remorselessly towards him.

She tried to step back, suddenly conscious of her near nakedness. 'Don't, it's not right. You're engaged to——'

'Shut up, don't keep reminding me,' he rasped, softness replaced in a flash by the cold ruthlessness she had glimpsed before. But the reminder saved her, for he released her and moved away. She was confused when he swung on to an entirely different tack. 'Emma,' he asked, 'who are your parents? I remember you corrected me when I referred to your father yesterday.'

'I never knew my real parents,' she admitted, relieved that he had thought better of his apparent intention to take her, half naked as she was, into another of his knee-buckling embraces.

'So who brought you up?'

'Foster-parents at first. Then I was formally adopted.'

'What were they like?'

'Terrific. I've been very lucky,' she said artlessly. 'My adoptive father was a history professor. I suppose that's why I enjoy rooting around old books, sorting out facts. The house was always littered with books. He died when I was sixteen, and I suppose if he'd lived it would have been easier to stay on at school and maybe go on to university. But Olga, that was my adoptive mother, took his death rather badly. Somehow I felt obliged to stay around until she got over him. And then suddenly it was too late. Look!' she exclaimed all of a sudden. 'Do you mind if I get dressed? I can't stand around chatting in nothing but bra and pants!'

'Don't get on your high horse again, Miss Frost. I'm not about to take advantage of you. I recall very well who you are at the moment. I'll give you ten minutes,' he went on briskly. 'Meet me down by the pool. The others were having a swim when I last heard. What would you like to drink? I'll have something ready for you before you leave.'

'I usually have cocoa at this time of night,' she told him, half joking. He gave a grimace and went out and she quickly donned her clothes, brushed her hair, and then, with a leaden heart at the thought of how close they were to saying goodbye, she made her way downstairs.

The others were still in the water, but they were out of earshot. Ripples of silver covered the surface as they swam and frolicked. Brick, his black tie unloosed, was sprawled in a white rattan chair when she arrived, and he got to his feet at once. 'You're Emma with a vengeance,' he said, slanting her a warm smile.

When she took her place in the chair opposite, not trusting herself to sit next to him, she noticed a silver pot on the table and two large mugs. He reached for the pot. 'Cocoa for Miss Frost. And, to express my gratitude for your sterling work this evening, I'll even join you.'

'Brick, is it really cocoa? You don't have to go that far!'

'There's an envelope here as well. I hope it's made all this worth your while.'

'No, I don't want anything. I got involved of my own free will——' She stopped. Even she didn't believe that. It was fate that had swept them together. And now it was fate sweeping them apart again. It didn't make sense. But there was still no need for Brick to feel he had to pay.

'I'm not arguing with you.' He poured two mugs of cocoa, and when Emma had sipped hers she realised it was more than just cocoa. It made some of the tension ease and she tried to enjoy these last few minutes together.

'Are you confident that Cosy will turn up in time?' she asked, drinking in the strong profile as reflections of silver light from the pool played across the perfect symmetry of his face.

He nodded, eyes glinting. 'If she has a shred of common sense she will. Otherwise——' he shrugged '—she's out. No two ways.'

'You're very hard.'

'I am?' His eyes were almost silver. They held hers in a steady gaze that sent shivers of desire scurrying up and down her spine.

'You seem so,' she managed to blurt. 'You don't make any allowances.'

'For what? Irresponsibility?'

Privately she thought he should have come to terms with this trait in his fiancée, if indeed it existed, and if he couldn't he should say so and find someone in keeping with his own standards. But she couldn't say this out loud. Instead she changed the subject. 'It's an odd coincidence that neither of us lived with our real fathers. I think that's what you said, isn't it? About Greg, I mean.'

He nodded. 'I don't know when he and Nancy adopted her.'

'Nancy?'

'Greg's wife.'

'You mean that wasn't her real mother either?'

He shook his head.

'That's very odd.'

'What do you know about your own people?' he probed gently. 'Anything at all?'

Emma frowned. 'My real name is Mills. I decided to take Olga's and Edwin's name of Andrews when I changed schools at fourteen. That's all I know.'

'I suppose Cosy must have what you call a real name. She's always used Greg's name as far as I know. It's just something that has never come up. I'll ask her what she knows when I see her again.'

'You mean you really do think there's something connecting us?'

'I'll ask her when I see her,' he repeated.

Emma dropped her glance. Soon it would be her look-alike, sitting here, dwelling perhaps with the same quiver of desire on the strong features of the man opposite. She felt a stab of jealousy but quelled it at once.

The phone lying on the table between them buzzed twice and Brick lifted it to his ear. 'It's Burt,' he said when he dropped it back. 'He's brought the car round to the front.'

She rose to her feet.

'It's still not too late to change your mind,' he told her huskily.

She shook her head. 'It simply wouldn't be fair. Lady Burley has already been let down once when the previous girl ran off to get married.'

'What about you?' he asked. 'Any chance of the same fate awaiting you?'

She gave a shaky laugh. 'No, thanks. I don't think I'm the marrying kind.'

His eyebrows shot up, but when she failed to enlarge on what she meant and instead began to head for the doors he sauntered along beside her, turning when she did to wave goodbye to the others.

Their cries of 'see you soon!' rang hollowly in her ears.

As they crossed the entrance hall to the main doors the phone on the marble console rang and Brick reached for it as he strode past. Then she saw him skid to a halt. His eyes took on an alert look and something told her who was on the other end of the line even before he said her name.

Her heart plummeted even though it had been a foregone conclusion what would happen.

'Cosy!' he was saying into the phone. 'Where the hell are you? Shall I come and get you? What?' His eyelids lowered.

Emma moved away. She couldn't hear the other side of the conversation and she certainly didn't want to listen in to Brick's side. He was telling Cosy what chaos her absence had wrought.

She must have asked what Brick was doing at
Rosedene, because as Emma reached the door she
heard him say, 'I came over to find you, of course.
Sybil was in a complete panic.'

Just then Burt came in. 'Ready, miss?' he asked.

She nodded. Brick was still on the phone and seemed
to have forgotten she existed. With a face like ice she
followed the chauffeur into the night. Soon she would
be safe home again, in what Brick had called her grim
little room. Well, so be it.

CHAPTER FIVE

IT HAD been about three o'clock by the time Emma had got to bed the previous night, and though she arrived at work on time she had been yawning her way through the morning. When Jack glided into the room in best butler mode, she jerked up, not realising it was coffee-time already.

But it wasn't. 'Telephone call for you, ma'am,' he intoned. Then glided out again.

She scrambled to her feet. 'Wait, Jack. . . Where do I take it?'

He popped his head back round the door. 'I'll switch it through, pet. Stay there.'

Puzzled as to who could be phoning her, she felt her heart begin to racket as she went to pick up the phone on the low table by the fire. There was a click, then a familiar drawl came down the line. She noticed her fingers tighten round the receiver and she sucked in a breath before steadying herself enough to reply in as near normal a voice as possible.

Brick cut in, 'You left that cheque behind. Not deliberately, I hope. I'm sending it on. Refresh my memory about your address, will you?'

Knowing it was no good arguing with him, she told him what he wanted to know. This is heaven enough—she was thinking—just to hear his voice again. Expecting him to ring off straight away, she was happy to find him staying on the line, chatting amicably about this and that, his voice lightly bantering, and sounding so close she could imagine his lips only inches from her ear. . . She could see him too, long legs sprawled out, phone in the crook of his shoulder, speeding along in the limousine perhaps, or sitting beside the pool, or in the gold and cream sitting-room at Rosedene Manor.

She would have asked him where he was if she had dared, but she was too shy to ask—as if a personal question would betray the depth of her feelings for him. It was better this way, she told herself. Friendly. He was obviously in such good spirits because Cosy was back. She dared not ask about Cosy and he didn't mention her either.

When he rang off, with no plans for seeing or even contacting her again, she fell back to earth with a crash. So he would pay her off and that was that.

Jack came in almost immediately with her coffee and then hovered, obviously hoping she would explain what was going on. 'Everything all right yesterday?' he asked when it was obvious she wasn't going to say anything. 'I was worried when I heard a complete stranger on the line asking about you.'

Emma tried to give a little smile, and then she said, 'It seems I have a double. He was sure I was his fiancée! It took some convincing to prove otherwise!'

Jack looked as if he wanted to pursue the matter, but Emma glanced at the pile of books on the desk as if eager to get on, only adding, 'That's all I know. I didn't meet her and I don't suppose I'm likely to. They live a very jet-set sort of life and they'll both be back on the other side of the Atlantic this time next month!'

Jack was satisfied with this, though he did say as he went out, 'You ought to follow it up. Just think if you found a long-lost twin! It'd be nice to have family of your own.'

Emma scowled to herself. If there was one thing she didn't want it was a family. And especially one that had anything to do with Brick Dryden and Cosy van Osterbrook. They weren't her type at all—at least, from what she'd heard about Cosy, they were as alike as chalk and cheese in everything except looks!

Next morning there was an envelope waiting for her in the morning post as she left for work. It was a cheque, she discovered when she ripped it open, neatly stapled to a thank-you card. When she looked at the amount it was for her eyes widened. He had said he would treble her day's pay, but this was ridiculous—how much did he imagine she was earning, for goodness' sake?

Stuffing it into her purse, she wondered what she would do with it. Flowers, she thought at once, flowers to brighten up the grim little room. And then she'd buy a couple of bottles of wine and invite Judy over for a slap-up meal. It would be good to cook a proper meal for once. And then, certain words ringing in her ears, maybe she'd splash out on a few clothes? Something to dazzle in. She frowned. Perhaps the clothes could be given a miss and she'd put the whole lot in the bank until she'd got over him and could be herself again.

It was nearly six by the time she got back that night, arms laden with daffodils and narcissi, so many of them they tangled in her hair, almost obscuring her face. She was just fumbling for her key when a voice made her spin. '*Brick!*' she exclaimed, nearly dropping her flowers at his feet.

'Here, let me.' He took her key and unlocked the door. She hesitated in the gloomy hall, drinking in with a shudder of pleasure the tough contours of his face, feeling their glances connect with the same familiar, knee-buckling impact as before. She turned away, reluctant to invite him up.

'I'm going back to Vancouver tomorrow,' he told her rapidly. 'I had to see you before I left.'

Had to? she repeated silently. It probably meant something urgent had come up. Something to do with Cosy. 'Did she come back safely?' she asked, her eyes searching his face, anticipating his reply.

'She's back all right.' His lips twisted. He took a step forward. 'Go up and put your flowers in water, then come and have a meal with me.'

'What, now?'

'Why not now?' he demanded tersely.

'I—well, I've not changed or anything,' she floundered.

'You look perfect as you are. Stop making excuses. You hadn't planned to go anywhere, had you?'

She shook her head, then noticed his eyes on the bottles of wine sticking out of her basket. 'I was going to ask the girl across the landing in for a meal. She's usually home on Fridays.'

He put a hand in the small of her back and turned her towards the stairs. 'I'll give you five minutes—or would you like me to come up and give you a hand?'

'Better not. It would ruin my reputation,' she tried to joke. Her spine still burning from his touch, she fled up two flights of stairs before she managed to slow enough to walk up properly. The flowers were thrown ignominiously into the sink, and as it filled with water she ran a comb through her hair and sprayed some perfume on her pulse-spots. Then, after almost forgetting to turn off the cold-water tap and half drowning the flowers in her haste, she tore back on to the landing. When she eventually descended and went into the street, Brick was leaning with an evident air of ownership against a low-slung sports car.

He gave a grunt of approval when she appeared. 'That was quick. Makes a change.'

'From what?'

He slid in beside her and gave her an enigmatic smile. 'From whom, you mean.'

Inserting the car into the stream of traffic with skilful rapidity, he drove towards the main road, leaving her no time to mull over the significance, if any, of this comment. It was peculiarly intimate sitting in the two-seater with him—its design was such that they were almost lying full length side by side, and she had enough to do to keep her mind from veering off into all kinds of wild fantasies.

She tried to fix on where they were going, and by the time they reached Hyde Park Corner she was already convinced they would carry straight on down Piccadilly into the West End. But instead he swung on to Park Lane, pulling up in the forecourt of the hotel on the corner. When they emerged from the car a man in livery came forward to park it and Brick ushered her briskly into the foyer. He was silent as he led the way to the lifts.

Assuming he was taking her up to one of the hotel restaurants, and wondering at his uncharacteristic silence on the way, Emma was surprised when they got out on the second floor and came to a stop outside one of the suites. He unlocked the door and ushered her inside.

There was someone already there, and as she stepped into the room Emma gave a gasp.

Poised beside the stereo on the far wall was a woman in a black and silver catsuit. She had her back to them as they came in, bending to insert a cassette into the machine, her long fair hair hanging loose, obscuring her face. But when she lifted her head to straighten up she looked squarely at Emma and she too gave a little gasp. Then her face, a face that was as familiar to Emma as her own, broke into an astonished smile.

'*My heavens*,' she drawled, 'he was *right*!' She moved forward until she was a few feet away then she halted, an expression of sharp curiosity mingling with deepening amazement on her face that Emma knew was the exact expression mirrored on her own face.

When Brick moved forward there was no need for his introduction. 'Cosy van Osterbrook.' The stranger who wasn't a stranger held out both hands with a delighted smile.

'Emma Andrews,' said Brick, pushing her forward. Emma reached out and Cosy gripped her hands in hers.

'I don't *believe* this! I can *see* it! But I do *not* believe it!' She walked round and round, looking at Emma from all angles with unabashed curiosity. 'What do *you* make of it, Emma? You worked it out yet?'

Emma shook her head. She hadn't spoken so far, but now she smiled and said, '*Can* we be twins? Is it possible? But no, surely not? I was born here in London and——'

'*Me too*!' Cosy took her by the arm. 'I was taken to Canada when I was eighteen months old. Greg and Nancy saw me in some orphanage and took me back with them. Couldn't have any kids of their own. They chose me. When's your birth date, Emma?'

'Sixth of June.'

Cosy shot a look at Brick. 'Isn't that *too* fantastic, honey! *The Gemini twins*!'

Brick's face held no expression whatsoever. Emma assumed it was because he had known before either of them that they must be twins. Now he went over to the bar. 'This calls for champagne at least,' he told them.

The two girls could only stare at each other, and Brick went to stand on the balcony as if to leave the moment to them both. Cosy took Emma by the arm again and led her to the sofa. 'This is the most amazing thing that's ever happened to me. It's great! What else do you know about your origins?'

'There's the name Mills on my birth certificate.'

Cosy nodded. 'That clinches it!' She threw her arms round Emma and gave her a hug. Then she hesitated. 'Have you ever tried to track your mother—our mother—down?'

Emma shook her head. 'I thought I might do some day. Discreetly, you know, until I saw how the land lay.'

Cosy nodded. 'I told myself I might give it a try once I was over here. That's why I came earlier than I needed. But,' she gave a grin, 'I kinda got distracted.'

They sat side by side on the sofa and Cosy told Emma all about her childhood in British Columbia, and Emma responded by telling her about being shunted from one set of foster parents to the next and finally, luckily, happily, she said, landing up with Olga and Edwin.

'I guess I've been the more fortunate in that I found my Olga and Edwin right away.' Cosy gave her another hug. 'Hey, this sure is going to take some getting used to! I *cannot* believe it. . .and have you thought of the pranks we can get up to?' She gave a wicked chuckle. 'I'm sure sorry we've missed all the fun of being kids in school! Were you any good in school?'

'Not bad,' admitted Emma.

'Me, I was always in trouble! You could have helped me out!' She turned her head. 'Hey, Brick, what about getting Emma to make this damned documentary for me?' She turned back. 'Are you in media too?'

Emma shook her head and explained how she had come to be working in the library at Lady Burley's.

'Sounds grim,' Cosy said sympathetically.

'Grim?' Emma felt her heart tighten. Cosy and Brick even shared the same vocabulary. '*I* like it,' she countered, 'though I can see you might not! But,' she went on, pulling a little face, 'it'll end soon. So I guess I'll be moving on anyway.'

'We'll get you something nice, don't you worry. Hey, Brick, what are you skulking out there on the balcony for? Come on in. Did you hear what I was telling her?' Brick appeared in the doorway, his glass of champagne empty. He looked from one to the other and his eyes came to rest on Emma.

Cosy got up and went over to him, lacing her arms around his neck. 'I said, honey, when she finishes working in that library we'll get her something a bit more exciting, huh?' She gave him a little peck on the cheek as if asking a favour.

'It's up to her,' replied Brick stiffly, his eyes still on Emma's. 'I'm sure there will always be work for her within one of the companies if she wants it.'

He disengaged himself from Cosy's arms and came over to Emma. '*Well?*' He crouched down in front of her so that his face was close enough to shut out everything else. 'How do you feel?'

'Speechless,' she muttered.

'Maybe I should have warned you. I thought you might refuse to come with me if you knew what I was planning. But I had to know if it was true. I couldn't leave tomorrow still wondering who you were, do you understand?'

She nodded. 'It's terrific,' she said in a flat voice. One part of her wanted to revel in the startling fact that she had a twin sister, but another part of her was dying at the thought that the only family she had was the fiancée of the man she herself had fallen for.

Cosy came up and put her hand on Brick's shoulder again. Emma saw the flash of an emerald and diamond engagement ring on one beautifully manicured hand.

'I bet we've got one hell of a lot in common underneath the surface,' Cosy was saying with a big grin on her face, and more accurately than she knew. 'I'm going to whisk you down to dinner right now and have a real good gossip. Brick, you can either get outta here or resign yourself to being ignored for once. This is our evening, hey, Emma honey?' She patted Emma on the shoulder. 'I *still* can't believe you're real. Come on, sister, we've got a *lot* of ground to cover!'

Brick rose to his feet as Emma got up. 'You two go down, then. I'll join you for liqueurs afterwards. Will a couple of hours be enough?' His eyes moved from one to the other.

'But are you going to dine alone?' Emma burst out. 'Surely on your last night here——'

'It's all right. I have plenty to keep me busy tonight. You go on down with Cosy. You've got a lifetime to catch up on.' He turned away.

Reluctantly, not wanting to miss a minute of their last evening together, Emma allowed Cosy to take charge. She guessed she was often in charge, and wondered what would happen when she met opposition. She couldn't help giving a little smile as the thought struck her, and when she caught Cosy's eye she said, 'This is going to be interesting! Do you think we'll be the sort of sisters who squabble—or real soul mates?'

'I talk straight from the shoulder, honey, and if you can get on with that I think we're going to do real fine.

Besides,' Cosy added, 'I've always wanted a partner in crime!'

Emma was unprepared for the impact their appearance made in the restaurant up in the roof garden. Cosy was obviously already known, and she was head-turning enough in her black and silver jump suit and the spiky high heels she wore. Emma felt like a mouse beside her in her plain cream-coloured blouse and calf-length tweed skirt. Luckily she was wearing a pair of tan court shoes and some decent stockings, though it was sheer chance she wasn't stomping around in brogues. But the fact that there were two of them caused an additional uproar. Cosy appeared to lap it up.

'Brick might have told us we were coming somewhere smart,' said Emma with a grimace when they were seated in the specific corner Cosy had insisted on. A bevy of waiters were vying to take their order.

Cosy laughed wickedly. 'I've had an idea for a fantastic spoof,' she said. 'Tell you later. But now I want to hear all about you so I've got an excuse to bend your ear with all my goings-on too.'

Over a delicious meal that Emma for one swallowed without awarding it the attention it deserved, they swapped likes and dislikes. Both had lived in the country, though admitted they probably preferred big cities, both liked travel, foreign food, discos, the colour turquoise and lobster thermidor. Neither was keen on freckles, hairdressers or men with beards. Emma admitted to liking classical music and reading. Cosy said she'd rather have a manicure and liked silk next to the skin.

When they got on to jewellery, Cosy flashed her ring and said how much she liked emeralds, and Emma admitted she probably would too, given the chance, but for the moment she was content with the plain gold locket Edwin and Olga had given her on her sixteenth birthday.

When she frowned, thinking of how soon after that poor Edwin had died, Cosy prised the truth out of her and told her that Nancy had died about then too.

'She was a real honey. Taught me all I know about how to handle men! Not that Greg needs handling. He's a poppet. Can't do enough for me.'

'Weren't you bothered about upsetting him when you disappeared?' asked Emma.

Cosy pouted. 'I guess you've been talking to Brick. He really tore me apart when I rang in last night. He tries to treat me like a little kid. Jawing on about showing a sense of responsibility. There's nothing wrong in taking off for a few days. Hell, I'm a free agent! He's been acting like a gaoler these last few weeks.'

'Isn't he simply worried about upsetting Greg's health?' Emma asked.

'So he says. Personally I think he's just keen to keep tabs on me.'

'I would have thought you'd want him to—I mean——' Emma broke off, confused '—given that you're going to be married and all that.'

Cosy gave a satisfied laugh. 'Maybe I do, but it doesn't mean I like to have him breathing down my neck. A girl needs time to relax. Brick wouldn't understand that. He functions in top gear all the time. It can take a lot of energy to keep up with a guy like him. Me,' she smiled, 'I'm just a blonde tabby that likes to lie in the sun while Brick, unfortunately, is nothing less than a big, predatory panther, never content unless he's stalking his next victim through the jungle.' Cosy glanced at Emma's ringless fingers. 'But what about you? No man in the offing?'

Emma shook her head. 'I'm not the settling-down type.'

Cosy laughed outright. 'Who are you kidding? I guess you mean the right guy hasn't shown yet. Wait until he does, you'll settle faster than a rattlesnake bites.' She leaned forward. 'Tell you what, you come back home with me and I'll fix you up with a real nice Canadian. Just tell me your type and I'll do the rest.'

'You're wicked, Cosy, you really are!' Emma couldn't help laughing. Then she lifted her head as a dark shape blocked out the light.

'Go away,' she heard Cosy say, 'this is strictly girl talk—I'm fixing Cinderella here for a hunky Canadian prince.'

Even before Emma looked up she knew what she would find—Brick's dark eyes gazing enigmatically into her own. He pulled out a chair as she averted her glance. 'Have you ordered coffee?' she heard him ask.

'Haven't ordered a thing, baby. These guys just keep bringing food and drink over.' It was true. They had been receiving first-class attention all night.

'You'll have to parade around in a twosome a lot from now on,' said Brick cynically. 'One of you is difficult to resist, two together could take over the world.' He gave a husky laugh. 'I'm sure you're already thinking of a way to turn it to your advantage, Cosy.'

The sting in the remark didn't hit home. Cosy matched his soft laughter with her own. 'You bet, honey. You know me.' She turned to Emma. 'We could halve the work on this documentary if you came in on it. *I* do some interviews, *you* do some.'

'But I can't. It's a skilled job——'

'Nothing to it,' corrected Cosy airily, 'you just have

to talk to people. The difficulty is getting them to shut up. Isn't that right, Brick?' Without waiting for his agreement, she went on, 'At least help me out with the boring research bits. You must know the scene over here better than any of us. You could really help out. Like with the sort of folk we could interview. What about this Lady Burley, for instance? Think she'd be willing to come over?'

Emma looked puzzled until Brick explained, 'I don't suppose Cosy's breathed a word about the assignment she's due to start at nine sharp tomorrow morning, but just to fill you in she's going to interview people over here and their counterparts in Canada, contrasting different lifestyles, values and so on.'

'Sounds interesting,' murmured Emma, trying to control the way her eyes wanted to drink him in. She rested one arm on the table and tried to look nonchalant.

'She'd be a great link for us,' judged Cosy, laying a hand on Brick's arm. 'Take her on the payroll as a researcher, Brick. I'd say she was indispensable!'

Brick's glance swivelled to Emma. 'Cosy's probably right, Emma.' His voice was as soft as a caress. 'I'd say you were probably indispensable too. . .'

His words, his tone, even the way he was looking at her, made her heart bucket. Then she told herself she was a fool when he added, 'The least you could do would be to keep an eye on Cosy. She's apt to be unpredictable—and that's putting it mildly. What do you say? Can you be persuaded?'

'I'm not quite sure what the proposition is,' Emma replied coolly. She would not be rattled by this man. Cosy's hand, adorned with its lovely ring, still rested on his arm. She was totally offside to be letting her feelings rampage out of control like this. She straightened in her seat. 'As you know, I'm already committed elsewhere.'

Brick held her glance, raising his eyebrows, the smooth hollows below his cheekbones more pronounced in the soft light of the restaurant. His eyes looked darker than ever, two slits, assessing her change of expression like a master card-player. She could see what Cosy meant by predatory. But why was she his victim, if indeed her feeling that he was waiting to pounce was correct? There was nothing she had that he could possibly want. Except to be a sort of minder for his fiancée while he was away.

She put this last thought into words and had the satisfaction of hearing them both laugh. 'Honey, if I wanted a minder I'd choose my own and he'd be a hunky, six-two body-builder,' Cosy shot a glance at Brick, 'though I've never liked second best in anything and——' here she reached over and kissed Brick on the lips '—you'd take a lot of beating, honey.'

'It shouldn't be difficult to find a substitute,' he replied lightly. 'I've always suspected you prefer brawn to brain, sweetheart.' He leaned back in his chair so that Cosy's hand slipped off his cuff. 'Why not sound out your Lady Burley, Emma? It's all fluid at the moment. The crew are simply getting as much on film as possible. The real job will be done back in the studio.'

He got up. 'I have to get back to Rosedene tonight, so I'd better not hang about here. Coming now with me, Emma? I'll drop you back home. No doubt you and Cosy will be getting together while I'm away. You can make up your mind later if you want to get involved.' His dark eyes seemed to hold hers, giving his last word a significance she knew she must be imagining. Involvement, in that suggestive, double-edged sense, was the last thing he could mean. She brushed a hand over her face.

'Yes,' she agreed with a cool smile fixed to her face. 'I suppose I'd better leave. It's been quite an evening.'

Cosy walked with them both to the exit and they all went down in the lift together. Emma was vibrantly aware of Brick's arm brushing hers as they stood pressed together, but fortunately Cosy kept up a constant stream of jokes and she had no need to do anything but keep a smile on her face.

'Check out your Lady Burley informally for me tomorrow, honey,' Cosy suggested as they made their farewells, adding warmly, 'and give me a ring here in the evening. I don't know what time we'll be through, but I'd like it if you'd come over and spend the evening gossiping again. We've only skimmed the surface.' She shot a glance at Brick. 'As usual, did I hear you say, sir?'

He gave a token smile. 'I didn't breathe a word.' He put a hand on Cosy's shoulder. 'Goodbye. I'll be in touch, of course. Take care.' He bent to kiss her on the lips. Emma turned away as she saw her twin sister bring up both her arms to twine them around Brick's neck. When she allowed herself to turn back, Brick was disengaging himself and she heard him saying, 'Be good. I want you to make the most of this chance, Cosy. Prove me wrong! That should give you some incentive!'

With that he came to the doors, and when Emma turned her last glance was of Cosy smiling at them both, a light-hearted smile on her face and not a trace of the regret she must be feeling at seeing her fiancé say goodbye.

The car was already waiting and as Emma slid in beside Brick she said, 'You knew, didn't you?'

'About your being twins?' He grimaced. 'It seemed obvious. Once you'd proved you weren't Cosy there was no other explanation.' He gave her a sidelong glance. 'You never did check out my passport as you threatened to.'

'I suppose the time for that has gone.'

'Hm,' he said non-committally, 'but it was a good enough ploy to persuade you to come out to Rosedene with me.'

She gave him a sharp glance, but he was already filtering into the unending stream of Park Lane traffic and his expression gave nothing away. She fell silent, wondering if the impression she had of both him and Cosy was correct. Certainly Cosy made no bones about the fact that she was interested in other men. Perhaps Brick had a similar free-wheeling attitude to women? Her lips tightened a little. On lots of levels she felt out of step with them both. This was just one of them.

When Brick pulled up outside the mansion block she unfastened her seatbelt straight away, but he put out a hand to stop her from getting out. 'Think about what Cosy said. I mean about—well,' his eyes raked over her face as if stripping it to the bone, 'about getting involved in any way you want—in *any* way,' he repeated. 'You only have to say. OK?'

'Any way?' she breathed with a lift of her eyebrows.

'Absolutely any way,' he replied swiftly, his eyes, hooded, fixed on hers.

She felt a blush begin to rise up her body and suddenly the small sports car seemed smaller still. 'I really don't think there's much future in—in my becoming involved, is there?' she stammered. She felt affronted, knowing full well that she wasn't mistaken about what he was driving at this time. It was outrageous.

He smiled a lazy smile and moved forward so that the light from the street lamp illuminated his face, bringing into stark relief the expression of cool amusement on it. One hand came up and gently brushed her lips. He said, 'I think there's a great future in it. You're going to have to accept that, Emma. Your life changed irrevocably from the moment we met. Don't fight it.'

She stiffened beneath his touch, wanting nothing more than to dash his hand away, but it was like being mesmerised when he held her glance like this. She felt trapped, an animal dazzled by the light. He was unfair to put her in this position. There was no doubt he knew what he was doing.

'I have no intention of becoming involved except in the most straightforward way,' she told him, stiffly. 'I can hardly turn my back on the fact that I've found my long-lost twin. But that family connection is the only one I want to pursue.'

She turned her head abruptly and began to reach for the door-handle, but he leaned across, deliberately close, his dark head brushing her chin. She felt the hair on the top of his head feather across her lips. They were still tingling when he moved back, the door swinging open. She made a dash for it, scrambling out as quickly as she could, but even then he was quicker and had got out and fronted the car even as she started to forge across the pavement towards the safety of the house.

He caught her by the elbow, swivelling her to face him so that he could kiss her lightly on the lips. Just as he had kissed his fiancée only minutes ago, she told herself furiously. She stepped back, wrenching her arm from his grasp.

'*Don't*. You can't pretend this time it's a case of mistaken identity!'

'Offended?' He laughed softly. 'But we're almost family, Emma. Don't be so frosty.'

'Have a good flight,' she clipped, jerking away. When she gained the top of the steps he was already heading for his car. He watched her from over the top of it as she scurried into the house. Then she slammed the door on him as if she couldn't get away fast enough—even though once on the other side she leaned against it until the sound of his car had faded into the night.

CHAPTER SIX

SOMEONE had pushed a note under Emma's door when she got in. It was Judy. It said, 'Was hoping to catch you tonight. Have had amazing feedback re your horoscope. If my light's still on when you get back, come on over! Love, Jude.'

Emma opened her door again and peered across the landing. No light. Guessing what the amazing feedback might concern, but mystified as to how Judy could have got on to it simply by looking at a few squiggles on a piece of paper, she went back inside and readied herself for bed. Brick's lip-prints were branded on her skin, but she despised him, she told herself. He was a faithless cad. It was a good job he and Cosy were two of a kind.

Next morning she bumped into Judy as they were both on their way to the launderette. 'I got your note,' she began, 'and if it's about having a twin I already know.'

Judy pulled a face. 'Dash it! Pipped at the post. I was dying to let you know.'

'But how on earth did you get on to it? There must be more in this astrology stuff than I dreamed of,' queried Emma as they walked down the street towards the launderette.

'That's probably true,' replied Judy, 'but the real give-away was the fact that your time of birth was noted. I didn't know it, but my astrology teacher tells me they always do that with multiple births. Are you the elder twin, do you know?'

'That's one thing we haven't discussed yet.' Emma gave a smile. 'No doubt we'll get around to it tonight,' and she went on to tell Judy the rest of the story, omitting only that part that laid undue emphasis on how she felt about her twin's fiancé.

Over the next few days she and Cosy got to know each other really well. It was a continual surprise to discover the things they had in common, even though, as Cosy herself admitted, they were as different as bagels and hamburgers when it came to some things. They agreed that such differences were an advantage rather than otherwise, and Emma was aware of a growing pleasure in the knowledge that she had an ally of some sort after so many years of feeling she didn't belong anywhere.

Despite their almost instant closeness, there was one thing she could never admit to Cosy, and whenever Brick's name was mentioned she knew she had to control the desire to open up about how she felt. It wouldn't be fair, and besides, she was coming to terms with her feelings now and feared it would cause needless upset if Cosy knew she felt anything for him other than the ordinary affection of a potential sister-in-law.

But the shared phone at home rang for her early one morning, just as she was cleaning her teeth. One of the tenants on the floor below knocked on her door to tell her.

Grabbing a robe, she whisked downstairs and nearly dropped the receiver when Brick's voice came melting down the line.

'I thought you were in Vancouver?' she demanded in a voice that sounded more like an accusation than a question.

'So I am,' he chuckled. 'Did I get you out of bed?'

'Not at all. What time is it where you are?'

'Midnight,' he told her. 'I'm just turning in after a hard day's work and wishing there were someone to turn in with.'

'I'm sure you'll survive until Cosy returns,' Emma admonished, feeling her hackles rise at the unmistakable invitation in his tone.

'Have you two cooked up anything between you yet?'

'Such as?' she demanded.

'As far as the documentary goes,' he said smoothly. 'What else?'

Not sure what he wanted to know, she said, 'I asked Lady Burley's secretary if she'd give us some time and she agreed. But she can't fit it in until the week after next.'

'That's OK, isn't it? How's Cosy's schedule shaping up?'

'I would have thought you'd know that better than I do,' she reprimanded. Surely he had spoken to Cosy by now?

There was a pause. 'Have you thought any further about getting involved?'

'In the documentary, you mean?' she replied swiftly. 'Yes, Cosy sort of persuaded me.'

'Maybe she'll persuade you to get involved on some other footing too,' he suggested with a meaningful chuckle. Before she could interject yet another reprimand he went on, 'She sure knows how to get her own way. But don't let her push you around.'

'Nobody makes me do anything I don't want to do, Brick. I thought I'd made that quite clear?'

'I'm pleased about the film anyway,' he replied, ignoring her last remark. 'I'll ring you again soon.'

The line went dead.

Not a man to waste words, she thought as she went

slowly back upstairs. She finished cleaning her teeth, and by the time she was ready to go out she was no nearer understanding why he had rung her before putting a call through to his fiancée. Maybe, she surmised, this was the way they ran their relationship—everybody at battle stations. Some couples were like that.

When she met Cosy the next day, Sunday, it was to go over some answers to a few questions she and the director, Jon, had been asking. Emma had met him briefly for the first time the second night she had dined with Cosy. He had come in after they finished eating much as Brick had done, but there the similarity ended. After pantomiming a double take when he met her, he had proved himself instantly likeable, but was as far removed in nature from a lethal panther as could be imagined. Short, thickset and easygoing, with straight brown hair in a stubby pony-tail, he put Emma in mind of a cuddly bear rather than anything more predatory. Emma had smiled when she met him. He was really sweet.

It was on the second time they met—on the Sunday morning—that she began to feel uncomfortable.

When she knocked on the door of Cosy's suite she heard a scuffling sound, then Jon himself came to open it. Cosy, Emma saw as she stepped inside, was still in bed, and, although she tried not to let her glance linger, it was obvious there had been someone else in the bed with her. Emma was embarrassed and angry on Brick's behalf, but she couldn't say anything. She knew Cosy would have given that throaty chuckle with which she dismissed any criticism and probably called her a silly prude into the bargain. They hadn't quarrelled yet, and Emma wondered how long they could last now without words being exchanged.

Jon was playing the good host, offering coffee and putting a piping hot croissant on to her plate. 'You keep very good time, Emma,' he observed. 'You said you'd be here at ten-thirty, and here you are on the dot!' He shot a glance at the still recumbent Cosy. 'Out of bed, girl, we've work to do.'

'I can talk just as well here as sitting over there with you,' replied Cosy, stretching out one hand for the coffee-cup that Jon had put within reach, and in doing so revealing the fact that she slept in the nude. 'And don't pig all those croissants yourself, Jon baby,' she went on. 'Bring some over to me.'

Emma watched him leap to obey and wondered what Brick's reaction would have been. She bit her lip. Poor Brick. She sipped her coffee and waited for the meeting, if that was what it was, to begin.

Somehow or other, she found herself roped in to joining the film crew later that week in an interview with a man who kept bees somewhere in Kent.

'Apparently,' said Cosy with a scandalised expression, 'he has no mains water, no electricity and no intention of ever obtaining them.'

'We'll pair him with a guy back home who lives two hundred miles from nowhere with a brown bear and draws his water from the river,' said Jon.

That night Brick rang again, and Emma told him all about it. When she finished he said, 'You sound as if you're really getting into things. That offer of a job still stands.'

'Don't be ridiculous, Brick,' she told him quickly. 'I couldn't work in Canada.'

'Why not?'

'Well,' she floundered, 'I just couldn't.'

He changed the subject and asked her how she was getting on with Cosy.

She was glad he couldn't see her face because it flushed at once, and she felt as guilty as if it had been she herself in bed with another man. 'I think she's going to turn in a really interesting film,' she said non-committally.

'With Roe's help,' came the reply. There was a tell-tale pause while she racked her mind for something neutral to say, but Brick went on, 'They're getting on all right, are they?'

'I—yes, I suppose so.'

'You don't sound very sure.'

'I don't shadow them all day,' she bit out.

'Nor all night either,' he remarked, and before she could add or contradict he went on, 'I may be coming over. I'll let you know.'

Again the line went dead.

That man, thought Emma angrily. He could do to learn some telephone manners. But underneath her annoyance was the worry that if he did turn up and found out about Cosy and Jon he was going to be very hurt and very angry. She wondered if the reason he rang her instead of Cosy was in order to keep a discreet eye on things—hoping, perhaps, that she would blurt out the truth he as yet only suspected. She felt angry to think she was being used in this way, and she wished with all her heart Cosy would run her life differently, or, if she couldn't, that she would keep everyone else out of it. Short of warning Cosy what Brick had said about coming over, there was nothing she could do.

Things came to a sort of head the following week. Brick's almost daily phone calls had continued, and to Emma's certain knowledge Cosy had received only a couple of calls in all that time. In some way it made it easier to excuse Cosy's playing around, for if Brick didn't care enough to make her feel wanted it was partly his own fault if she was two-timing him. But Cosy could be difficult, as she soon proved.

The interview with Lady Burley went off remarkably well and Cosy heaved a sigh of relief. 'Now maybe I can get on with a little living,' she remarked as the crew started to pack their gear and she and Emma somehow found themselves sitting in the kitchen with Jack and the rest of the kitchen staff. Cosy had started to flirt outrageously with Jack, who was as fascinated as people always were when they came face to face with a pair of identical twins.

Emma had lifted her head at Cosy's last remark. 'Don't forget you've got that interview with the keeper of the transport museum tomorrow. Then you can think of having a rest.'

'Emma, honestly, you're a slave-driver just like Brick. If I want time off, I shall sure as hell have it!' she drawled. 'I'm not bound by anybody.'

'But you are bound by an agreement. First to the crew and second to Brick. He expects everything to be completed when he turns up the day after tomorrow.'

'Tough.' Cosy stuck out her lower lip. 'You think she's a workaholic too, don't you, Jack baby?' She turned a dazzling smile on the smitten butler. He was too loyal to agree outright, and he managed to say something designed not to offend either of them, but Cosy immediately took it as a sign of support.

'There you are, Emma. Jack agrees with me. And what I suggest, if you're so bothered about letting anybody down, is that you take my place. You're far more interested in this aspect of it than I am, and you know the ropes by now. You do it if you're so worried, and let me have a well-earned rest.'

'Don't be ridiculous——' began Emma.

'Well, why not?' challenged Cosy, her eyes spark-
ling, any animosity at being pulled up by Emma
forgotten as the idea took hold. 'Nobody would know
the difference if you wore my clothes. I've been dying
to swap places ever since we met——'

'You'd hate to swap places with me and you know
it,' observed Emma bluntly.

'I wouldn't mind you swapping places with me,' Cosy
replied bountifully. 'In a way it would mean we could
have double the fun!'

Emma lifted her eyes skywards. 'Tell her she's crazy,
Jack, please.'

Just then Jon came in and Cosy at once changed the
subject. This was deliberate, as Emma found out later
that evening. There was a phone call. It was Cosy.
'Sugar, I'm lying in bed with a real bad migraine. I
knew it was coming on, that's why I tried to back out
of the shoot tomorrow. Please, be a real sister and take
over for me? It's only a few minutes' footage in the
final thing. You can do it standing on your head, you
know you can.'

'Cosy, I'm not sure I believe this story about your
migraine,' Emma began.

'Emma, you know something? You can be real
mean. If you knew how rotten I was feeling right now,
you wouldn't have the heart to say such a thing. I've
already sent over the clothes I'd have worn for conti-
nuity,' she went on, ''cos I never expected you to say
no. All you have to do is turn up at the museum at
eleven. From there it's plain sailing. And you know
how much you like museums,' she added. 'You'll be
able to poke around behind the scenes to your heart's
content.'

Emma frowned. 'You're a real ace at organising
people, Cosy.'

'Thank you. I regard it as my greatest talent. I knew you'd be fair.'

'I didn't say I——'

'You perfect person!' Cosy went on. 'Thanks a bundle. I'll tell Jon. He'll be over the moon.' She rang off.

That's another thing they have in common, thought Emma crossly. They both ring off as soon as they've delivered their orders. About twenty minutes later a parcel of clothes arrived by special courier, and Emma reluctantly gave in to the inevitable.

Next morning she found herself outside the transport museum at eleven sharp. Jon rolled up a few seconds later. 'Never known you be on time before,' he greeted her, taking her by surprise by pecking her on the cheek. He put an arm round her waist, 'How's the head?'

Emma sighed. 'It's me, Jon. Emma.'

He peered into her face and she felt his arm slide away. 'I'll have to take your word for it.' He peered closer still. 'You're not making a mockery of me are you, Cosy? I never know what you're up to.'

'Emma, actually,' she said, walking briskly into the entrance.

Later, as they wound things up, she had to admit she'd enjoyed it. She hoped her accent wouldn't come over as too much of a difference after what had gone before, but guessed that most of what she said would be edited out anyway, leaving only the answers her questions had elicited.

Still wearing the suit Cosy had had sent round for her, she decided to call in at the hotel with Jon to see how Cosy's so-called migraine was progressing. When they arrived there was no one in the suite, however, and someone on Reception said Miss van Osterbrook had been seen leaving the hotel around mid-morning. Jon ran a hand over his face. 'Now I know it's you, Emma. I've had my doubts all day. She's been practising your accent, you know.'

'I hope you find her soon.' Emma made a hurried goodbye, not wanting to get any more involved than she had to. She was just cutting across the foyer with the intention of catching a bus home when there was a sound behind her and she turned in time to see a lethally familiar shape detach itself from one of the armchairs and head towards her.

'Hi, sweetheart,' he greeted her, soft-voiced and dangerous. It was Brick. He seemed to loom over her, something menacing in his manner—as if expecting the worst, she told herself. He clamped a hand on her shoulder. 'Going somewhere?' He shot a meaningful glance at his watch.

Before she had a chance to extricate either herself or Cosy, there was a loud greeting and Jon hurried over. He shook Brick by the hand. 'Didn't expect you until tomorrow,' he said cheerfully. 'But this is great. I wanted a word with you. What about having a nightcap in the bar?' He gave Emma a wink. 'No need to worry,' he said affably, 'everything's under control.'

'You two still on speaking terms?' asked Brick, looking from one to the other.

Emma's heart went out to him. Surely Jon must feel a pang of remorse at playing such a double game?

'You're just going back up, are you?' Jon asked with special emphasis that made no sense to Emma whatsoever. She was still trying to work out what to do when both men moved off. She waited until they were out of sight, then turned and hurried outside. What would Brick do when he found Cosy missing yet again?

Especially after he had apparently just met her in the hotel foyer? It crossed her mind that she could help Cosy out by dashing up to the suite and impersonating her, but the idea was too preposterous, especially when she imagined what might inevitably follow after Brick had greeted his fiancée! She couldn't assume that it was a platonic relationship, just because Cosy had a lover.

Sickened, she made her way home as quickly as she could, impatient with every halt of the bus, and she was eventually back in the relative calm of her own room, thankful that, even if it was 'grim', everything that happened in it was as straightforward as could be.

Carefully hanging Cosy's suede suit in the wardrobe, she changed into a towelling robe and made herself a mug of cocoa. Then she settled down in front of the gas fire with a magazine. The twists and turns of the day had left her feeling restless, not least being that unexpected meeting with Brick just now. Much to her annoyance, he still exerted the same hold over her desires, and she was furious to find her emotions taking control again, whizzing her on to the now familiar roller-coaster, so that all she could do was to hold on, despite every sickening lurch towards imminent catastrophe.

Her ruminations were disturbed when there was a knock on her door. Judy, she guessed, getting to her feet. Maybe a good heart-to-heart was exactly what she needed. She opened the door with a flourish, a smile already on her face. Then she froze.

'May I come in? Or was that smile meant for some other late-night visitor?'

'*Brick*!' she gasped. 'Did anybody see you come up?'

'Only the old fellow on the ground floor. He seemed kind of understanding about it.'

'How *could* you?' She stepped back and Brick took

it as an invitation to step inside. 'Why have you come here?' she demanded, continuing to back away.

'Some welcome, I must say. I fly seven thousand miles and all you can say is, "Why have you come here?"'

'I appreciate the fact that you've had a long flight, but you didn't come all this way to see me, so I feel that in the circumstances I'm quite justified in asking what you're doing here—in my bedsit, at this time of night.' Her tone was sharp.

He put his hands in the pockets of his leather flying jacket and simply smiled at her. There was a moment's suspense when Emma didn't know what to expect, then somehow his arms were around her and his lips were searching out her own, his mouth hot with unmistakable desire, his urgency annihilating her resistance in seconds.

'Hell, I've dreamed of this moment ever since I flew out. Have you missed me too?' he demanded harshly. 'Say you've thought of me now and then, Emma, say it.'

He enveloped her mouth again, prising her teeth apart before she could reply, his tongue coaxing an ever more helpless response from her with every tiny movement. He arched her back, one hand pressing her pelvis against his own, the other sliding inside the front of her robe to fondle her breasts, his touch driving her to a pitch of longing she had never imagined. Her senses were on fire and she moaned deep in her throat as her own hands came up, her fingers lacing through the thick crop of black hair as if to hold him against her forever. But a voice was already crying to be heard. It warned her that what she was doing was wrong. When his hand slid down between her breasts, lowering to the tender skin of her stomach then lower still, she fought a battle with her conscience and bit by bit her conscience began to win.

'Brick, this isn't right,' she protested, averting her head even as her body began to open to him.

He was bleary-eyed as she pushed against him with both hands. She would never move that bulk of muscle and purpose, she thought, bringing both hands over his face, her fingers gouging into the skin over the hard bones of his cheek and jaw.

He jerked his head back, catching both her hands in one of his, but it was enough to allow her to twist away.

Dragging shut the front of her robe, she turned on him, the heat of her shame bringing a hectic colour to her cheeks, but before she could speak he broke in roughly, 'Don't pretend. We both want it, Emma. You know it!' He fingered his cheek where her fingernails had scrawled their protest.

'No, Brick. It's Cosy you want. Remember her? Your fiancée? Now get out! Before I call for help!'

'Help?' He shook his head as if to clear it from some bad dream. 'Help's the last thing you need. You manage very well by yourself. But I wonder why you suddenly had second thoughts?'

'It would be obvious if you had an ounce of imagination,' she hissed. 'I'll give you three seconds to get out.'

'Three?' He raised his eyebrows, a smile of total self-confidence playing over his features. Then deliberately, taking his time, he strolled over to the armchair she had recently vacated and sat down in it as if he owned it. 'I'll go,' he told her, 'when I'm good and ready. Now, aren't you even going to offer me a drink after coming all this way to see you?'

'You must be mad! I'd rather offer a drink to a rattlesnake.'

'Snakes are quite nice creatures. You obviously haven't met many——'

'One is enough,' she came back. 'But I can understand your fellow feeling very well.' She gave a short laugh. She knew full well why he had turned up at her door—because Cosy hadn't been there to greet him. 'I don't know what came over me just now. You shouldn't read too much into it. It'd be best if you forgot it ever happened.'

'What came over you was honest-to-goodness desire. Nothing wrong with that. And if you seriously expect me to forget it you must be mad.' He gave an amused laugh, dark eyes travelling with deliberate slowness over her flushed face. 'Even now a part of you is wondering why you're not in my arms, in that bed so conveniently close at hand.'

She cast a fearful glance over her shoulder, as if it could entice her by its mere proximity into his arms.

'Seems a shame to let it go to waste,' he murmured, his eyes still raking her from head to foot.

'Please, Brick. You're being unfair. You know you're only here because you don't have Cosy to go to.'

'What makes you say that? I've already said hello to Cosy.'

She didn't call him a liar, but her eyes were eloquent with disbelief.

He went on, 'Admittedly it was a rather brief hello, but I felt I had more to say to you than to her at this time of night.'

'What do you mean?'

He gazed at her for a long moment, a slow smile overspreading his face. 'Isn't it obvious?' he demanded at last, in a voice that was clogged unmistakably with desire.

Emma frowned. 'The only thing obvious about you, Brick, is your aim to find a substitute lover for the night.'

'If that's what's coming over we'd better backtrack, start again. My thoughts have got way ahead of yours since I've been away. That much is clear. Foolish of me not to guess. I thought by ringing you every night we'd be able to keep pace with each other. Well,' he went on, 'that can't be helped. What about sharing that mug of cocoa with me? It is cocoa, isn't it, Miss Frost?' He reached forward and picked up the mug standing in front of the gas fire.

She didn't know what to do. Her impulse was to get him out of her bedsitter as soon as possible, yet something held her back. She knew what lay in wait for him tomorrow when he finally caught up with Cosy. The truth must surely come out because, from what he had said over the phone, he already suspected something was wrong. Knowing him as she did, he would confront Cosy with it tomorrow—and knowing Cosy as she did, she wouldn't hedge. Emma couldn't doubt that Brick was only seeking solace here now because not only did she look like his erring fiancée, the woman he really loved, but she also seemed to be available and vulnerable to his particular brand of appeal.

'Oh, honestly,' she groaned half to herself, 'I can't make sense of this. I just want you to leave.'

'It's very simple,' he told her. 'I'm on my way to Rosedene. Do you want to come?'

She shook her head. 'What about your fiancée? Surely you'll want to see her first thing in the morning?'

'She'll be coming down with Roe, I expect.'

She was astonished at his complacency. Did he have

to throw them both together? Her thoughts flashed
back to Jon's aside in the foyer of the hotel when he
had told her everything was under control. Then he
had told Brick he wanted a word with him.

Now Brick went on, 'They seem to be on speaking
terms again. I must admit you had me worried when
you sounded so dubious over the phone.'

'Is that the reason you flew back earlier than
expected?' she asked with a sudden pang.

He rested his head on the back of the chair and
closed his eyes. It gave Emma a chance to let her eyes
dwell with love and compassion on the tough, hard
lines of his face. He didn't have the appearance of a
man close to heartbreak, but then she guessed he
wouldn't be the type to wear his heart on his sleeve for
anyone. And maybe, in fact, he knew less than she
imagined. She longed to be there when he learned the
truth in case he needed her, but she knew she would
find it almost impossible to remain dispassionate when
her own heart would be breaking too.

His eyelids flickered open. 'I must be more tired
than I thought,' he observed. 'Wish I'd asked Burt to
meet me now. Can't say I relish the drive out to
Rosedene. . .alone. . .' His eyes swooped towards the
single bed in the corner of the room. 'Pity it's so small.
I'd suggest you let me borrow it for the night. It looks
inviting. . .'

'You know I have to say no.'

'To start with, yes. But that's only because you're so
well brought up, Miss Frost. I reckon I could bring you
to change your mind if I set my mind to it. . . I guess I
could get you to do exactly what I want—and make
you want it too.'

Emma froze. Here she was, oozing secret compassion for him, and all he could do was calculate her

availability! Really, he and Cosy deserved each other.
She didn't know what to do next.

She couldn't stand there all night waiting for him to
make up his mind to leave. He might go on sitting
there in front of the gas fire for hours. But nor could
she sit down. Not on the floor near the fire, because
that would bring her too dangerously near to him. And
not on the bed either. Certainly not on the bed. She
cursed her grim little room with its lack of furniture
and shifted on to the other foot. She ought to throw
him out.

He saved her from the decision by rising to his feet.
'It's a snug little place. I could fall asleep here quite
happily. But that, Miss Frost, would no doubt drag
your reputation into the mud and I would hate to do
that to you.'

He moved to the door. 'I'm glad I've seen you. I had
to make sure you were still real and not something I
dreamed up last time I was over here. Come down to
Rosedene at the weekend. I'll send a car for you at ten
o'clock Saturday morning. We'll be showing the rushes.
I promise not to touch you at all without a formal
invitation. How's that? And, Emma, even if you don't
trust me, don't let that stop you from coming. Remember, there's safety in numbers.'

With a lift of his hand, he turned the latch and went
out. Emma sank to her knees in front of the fire and
wrapped her arms tightly round herself for protection.
There was no way she was going to Rosedene at the
weekend. It was a complete impossibility. . . It would
be like walking into a lion's den.

CHAPTER SEVEN

FIRM in her intention to have nothing more to do with Brick Dryden beyond the mere family obligation of treating him with the distant politeness of an in-law, when Cosy rang her at work the next morning Emma carefully avoided any mention of his weekend invitation.

'Jon tells me you got on brilliantly yesterday,' Cosy began. 'I knew you could do it. In all fairness I think you're the one who's cut out to play the role Brick wants. I get real bored having to ask a load of serious questions. I'm not cut out for documentaries and he knows it.'

'I really don't think it's my sort of thing either,' replied Emma at once.

'But it is! It really is!' Cosy insisted. 'You're scared right now because you're dazzled by it and it's all new, but once you get used to the idea you'll be flying!'

'Listen, Cosy,' Emma began carefully, 'I'm glad I managed to help you out yesterday, even though I think you had a bit of a cheek forcing the issue the way you did, but our lives, our aims, despite a lot of similarities, are really very different.' She paused, choosing her words carefully. 'I'm going to be quite busy over the next week or so——' she estimated that would cover the length of Brick's stay in England '—and I'm not going to be able to see as much of you,' and Brick, she added silently, 'as I would like——'

'Hey, hold it right there. I'm going home soon. You mean you're intending to leave it right where it is? You *can't* be serious! Now we've found each other we can't just switch each other off! Hell, we're sisters—*twins*—and you can't get much closer than that! Come off it, Emma, you don't mean this, do you?'

Emma hadn't expected Cosy to be so vehement. 'I do—I mean—what I mean is. . . I don't want to cut myself off from you, of course I don't. . .but you must see how difficult things are?' She didn't know how to explain without dragging Brick and his importuning into it.

But Cosy at once jumped to conclusions. 'You're mad at me because of yesterday,' she complained. 'I guess you have a right to be annoyed. I know I should have let you in on it without spinning a line about a migraine, but you're more honest than me—I suppose I thought you might spill the beans to Jon if he asked you outright what was going on. Hell, though, you must understand, I hate being tied down to anyone—even when my feelings are one hundred per cent engaged. I just felt, well, I wanted to get away. Actually,' she sounded contrite, 'I went ice skating with Jack and some of his mates.'

'Mates?' Despite herself, Emma smiled at the anglicism.

'It was real good fun. I promised to teach him when I was over there with you all at Lady Burley's. You're not going to be prim and proper about a little thing like that, are you? It couldn't have been more innocent, more's the pity!'

Emma couldn't help smiling. 'You're hopeless, Cosy. Do you realise how furious Brick would be if he knew you dodged out of an assignment to go *ice skating*?'

'Hey, you're not going to snitch on me, are you, honey? Be a pal!'

'Did you tell Jon?' she asked.

'Afterwards, yes. I knew there was no point in telling him first because he'd've hit the roof. Listen,' she went on, 'that's all past history now. When are we two going to get together to plan the future?'

Emma made a quick decision. 'The future's cut and dried as far as I'm concerned, but if you're leaving soon let's meet for lunch and plan the next few days.'

'You're on.' Cosy sounded pleased and they quickly arranged to meet at a café within a few minutes from where Emma was working.

She replaced the receiver with a smile. Cosy was hopeless. But at least they had skirted the tricky problem of Brick without the need for any outright untruths. With care she would be able to do the same until they both went home.

It was Friday and the restaurant was busy when, later that morning, Emma made her way to their appointed meeting. She was surprised to find Cosy already waiting in the cocktail bar.

'I can't believe it!' She greeted Cosy with a hug.

'Jon was singing your praises so I thought I'd better take a leaf out of your book and learn to be on time. You sure seem to manage to make yourself popular with the guys—without even trying!' Cosy patted her arm. 'I felt a bit sorry for you when we first met. Saw you as a Cinderella figure. I could see you were having a hard time making ends meet, but you know, Emma, I guess you make out pretty well in your own way.' She stopped and bit her lip. 'Does that sound patronising? It's not meant that way.'

'It was damned patronising,' said Emma with a grin, 'but I forgive you. You wouldn't expect anything less, would you?' Still smiling, she followed Cosy to a table for two.

'Now, then, my plan is this,' said Cosy as soon as they were seated. 'When you come out to Rosedene this weekend——'

'Wait a minute, who said I was coming out there?'

'Brick, of course. He called round to see you last night, didn't he?' Emma's eyes widened and Cosy went on, 'I'd just got into bed when he arrived. I was having a chat to a guy down the corridor when you and Jon came back last night. That's how I came to miss you. Brick told me he was driving back to the house and calling in on you on the way——'

So he had seen Cosy after all. Emma broke in, 'I told him I couldn't make it this weekend.'

'This morning when he rang he sounded confident you could—in fact, he suggested Jon and I stay in town an extra day then come down with you in the limo.'

Emma scowled. 'You two,' she grumbled. 'You really like to get people organised, don't you?' She registered that Brick was as complacent as ever, leaving Cosy to Jon's attentions, but Cosy had picked up her last remark.

She laughed. 'I don't see me as organising people for the power it brings. I don't look at it like that—I'd say we like to help people do the things they secretly want to do but haven't the courage to start!'

'I can assure you, in my case courage has nothing to do with it. Put simply, Rosedene is the last place I want to spend the weekend,' Emma burst out.

Cosy looked startled. 'Why the hell not? It's a gorgeous place.' She peered closely into Emma's face and demanded, 'Is there something you haven't told me?'

Emma felt her lips tighten.

'Well?' demanded Cosy. 'Out with it. You can't have secrets from me. I'm your twin sister.'

Emma looked down. 'I just don't get on with Brick,' she admitted, going as close to the truth as she dared. 'I find him arrogant and overbearing. He rides slipshod over everyone and on top of that he seems to think he's God's gift—I mean, I just don't *like* him.' Forgive me, she prayed. It was almost true. She didn't like him. Her feelings were too wild for mere liking. But that was something that was definitely going to remain a secret. Twin sister or not.

'I didn't realise.' Cosy frowned. 'I can't argue with what you say. He *is* arrogant. He *is* overbearing. And,' she smiled faintly, 'he not only thinks he's God's gift— he damned near is!' She looked dreamy. 'He's got the most perfect body of any man I've ever seen. Plus a mind like a steel trap. He's also one of the *kindest* men I know. . .' She shot Emma a careful glance. 'Maybe he finds it difficult to let you know how he feels? It must be pretty shattering for him to find somebody who looks exactly like me. I mean, what do you make of a thing like that? What do you *feel*?'

Emma was silent. She knew what Brick felt. Lust. Pure and simple. It was an age-old male fantasy to take two identical women to bed, wasn't it? She shuddered. 'I take your point about how confused he must be feeling,' she admitted, 'but I still don't relish the prospect of spending a weekend idling around Rosedene.' She shrugged. 'It's unreal,' she explained, searching for some excuse that would carry conviction. 'Besides, I have things I want to catch up on.'

'Like a good book or something?' Cosy laughed. 'There's a fabulous library at Rosedene. You want to get Brick to show you round. Then get him on the topic of the minor English poets. He read humanities at university. He's a real clued-up guy. That's another thing we don't share!'

'Another? I thought you had a lot in common?'

Cosy gave a wicked chuckle. 'In some ways, yeah, we've got a whole lot going for us,' she shrugged, the gleam still in her eyes, 'but in other ways,' she finished, 'forget it!'

Emma could just imagine the stormy marriage that lay ahead. She didn't know where her sympathies lay. 'I can't come, anyway,' she said emphatically, 'so that's that.'

Saturday morning it was pouring with rain. Emma bumped into Judy as she was lugging her week's washing downstairs to the launderette. Judy laughed and pointed to her own bundle. 'I live for the day when I have a nice kitchen complete with automatic washing-machine,' she joked. They walked down to the launderette on the corner and Emma kept an eye on Judy's washing and she did likewise while each popped down the road to do their weekend shopping.

'I've been meaning to ask you over for a meal,' explained Emma when they met up again beside the driers, and she went on to outline the events of the past few days. 'Meeting Cosy makes me even more sceptical about astrology,' she said candidly. 'We two couldn't be more different beneath the surface.'

Judy nodded. 'You probably have different ascendants,' she pointed out. 'The stars don't stay the same for long. You're Pisces. She could be Aries.'

Emma smiled. 'Maybe that explains it!' She told Judy about the weekend invitation and found she could be more open about her muddled feelings for Brick than she could with Cosy, and, feeling better for having got some of it off her chest, she eventually accompanied Judy back to the house. Rain was still gusting down the street and Emma had her head bent against it as she hurried in towards the front steps.

'Hey, about time! Where the hell have you been?' A hand on her shoulder made her pivot.

'Brick! I thought you were in the country! What are you doing here?' She glared up at him with rain streaming down her face, hair hanging in rats' tails, the very opposite of Hollywood glamour.

'I've been sitting in the car waiting for you for about an hour,' he told her irritably. 'I said ten, remember?'

'And I said no!'

'What the hell have you been up to?'

'I've been at the launderette,' she told him, raising her chin, 'a place you've probably never even heard of.'

'Get in the car.'

'What?'

'You're coming to Rosedene whether you like it or not. I told you what time you'd be picked up. . . And hurry up about it,' he added, 'we're both getting wet, standing out here.'

By now Judy had walked up.

'I am not coming to Rosedene. Ever. Get that straight!' Emma bit out.

'Like hell!' he gritted, ignoring Judy's startled expression and reaching for the bag Emma was carry-ing. 'What the hell *is* this?'

'My week's washing, do you mind?' Emma made to grab it back.

'I'll take it in for you,' said Judy swiftly. She took it from Emma's nerveless fingers and walked up the steps to the door with it.

'I'm glad your friends have a bit of common sense,' he growled. 'Now get moving.'

'Judy, bring me back that washing—I——!' Emma

swivelled from one to the other, finishing up face to face with Brick. 'How many times do I have to tell you? I am not coming to Rosedene so long as you're there! So you may as well climb back into that flashy car of yours and drive on, buster!'

'Resorting to Americanisms, eh?' He gave a satisfied chuckle. 'Should stand you in good stead when you come to deal with interviewees in the future.'

She threw back her head and gave a hoot of laughter. 'If you believe what Cosy's been saying you're crazier than I thought! I never said I was going to join the fabulous Dryden empire, as an interviewer or in any other capacity,' she added meaningfully. 'Would you like me to put it in writing?'

Judy was at the top of the steps by now. 'I'm going in, Emma. See you on Monday morning. Have a nice weekend!' She was grinning from ear to ear and Emma was stupefied by her instantaneous betrayal. Judy *knew* how she felt about this man—she'd just spent half an hour in the launderette telling her! But the door opened and Judy slipped inside with a last rather envious glance at Brick.

Emma didn't intend to waste time bandying words on the front step. If he wanted to stand there in the pouring rain, that was up to him. *She* was going in. She took out her key and inserted it in the lock, but before she could push open the door he was beside her and the key was being ripped from the lock and she heard the latch drop on the other side.

'Give me that back! How dare you?' She turned on him in fury.

He was laughing humourlessly and jigged the key in one hand just out of reach. 'I'm keeping this until Monday morning. You won't need it until then. You're coming with me.'

'Give it *back*!' she demanded furiously.

He slipped it into his inside breast pocket. 'If you want it,' he said dangerously, 'come and get it!'

'*You*——' Words failed her. Then she recovered and thrust herself forward. 'You arrogant devil! What game do you think you're playing? You and Cosy are a real pair—you thoroughly deserve each other! Now stop trying to order me about and give me my key!'

'No.'

'*What*? How *dare* you? I'll—I'll——'

'Shout all you want,' he remarked steadily, 'but this time I'm not playing. I want you to see the rushes before we leave. Cosy wants you to. She values your opinion. And,' he added, though she didn't believe him, 'so do I.'

Her answer was to turn back to the front door and press her finger long and hard on the top bell. Judy was probably the only one in at this time on a Saturday, and she would come down and open the door. She must.

But there was no sound from within no matter how hard she pressed the button, and Brick, seeing what had happened, knew she was locked out. 'Isn't it crazy to stand here in the pouring rain when there's a warm welcome awaiting you in a pleasant country house filled with friends?' he informed her. 'If you have any sense you'll accept defeat for once and make the best of things. Surely you want to see your twin sister before she flies back home?'

'I can see her next week,' Emma muttered, uncomfortably aware of how reasonable his proposition sounded, put like that.

He raised his eyebrows. 'But she's leaving first thing on Monday morning. How can you see her?'

'She said soon. She didn't say Monday.'

'Monday is soon.' He took her by the elbow. 'Come on, Emma,' he said on a more conciliatory note. 'You want to see the film, don't you?'

She was silent, opposition still warring within her.

'Come on, sweetheart. I gave you my word the other night. I won't lay a finger on you. And Cosy, Jon, everybody will be disappointed if you don't turn up. Cosy's been on the line to Greg already. He's doing fine and she told him all about you. He's planning to ring this weekend specially to say hello——'

'That's really cheap of you, Brick, using a sick old man as leverage,' she told him. Her face was set in a mutinous expression, rain still slashing against her cheeks. She blinked to flick the raindrops out of her eyes. Brick was soaking wet too now, not that that was any consolation.

He gave a small shrug. 'I'm not using him. It just happens to be true.' He put his head on one side, waiting for her answer, a hint of challenge in his eyes that made her flinch with annoyance. Did he think she dared not spend the weekend with him? That she was frightened she couldn't trust herself to withstand his seductive attentions? She wouldn't put it past him. He was conceited enough.

'I'll have to go back in to get some clothes,' she told him, a faint expectation that if she could get her key back she could probably barricade herself in her room until he gave up and went away. But he didn't fall for it.

'You don't have to go in for a thing. Not with all Cosy's gear, most of it unworn, bursting from the cupboards.'

'You seem to expect me to share *everything* of Cosy's,' she said as cuttingly as she could.

He grimaced. 'Nasty.'

'*Don't* you?' she persisted.

'Not everything. . .no.' He took her by the arm again. 'Come on, stop wrangling and let's go. We can talk just as well in the car and at least it's dry.'

Resigned to the fact that she wasn't going to get away, she allowed him to lead her to the car. As she strapped herself in she tried to shut her mind to the miles of silence that lay ahead, for one thing was certain: she wasn't going to be the one to make light conversation. She would accompany him, but she would make sure he was aware it was by no means willingly.

However, he drove straight to the hotel in Park Lane, and to her surprise Cosy and Jon were waiting for them, and as soon as they got out of the sports car the limo turned up and the four of them piled into the back.

Cosy nipped her arm. 'I knew you'd change your mind. Brick was so sure you intended to join us.'

Saved from the experience of having to be alone with Brick throughout the journey, Emma didn't mind making herself agreeable to Cosy and Jon, but she still pointedly ignored Brick, even though she knew Cosy noticed and gave her one or two swift glances.

When they eventually arrived at the manor she whispered in Emma's ear, 'You're being very hard on him.'

Emma gave her a scathing glance. 'As he virtually kidnapped me I think I'm being remarkably lenient.' Not bothering to explain, she walked on into the house, only wishing she could get through the weekend as quickly as possible. But with Brick, herself, and then Cosy and Jon present, she couldn't help wondering how long it would be before the balloon went up.

It had been right on lunchtime when they arrived, and even Emma had to admit there was a lavish spread ready for them. It certainly beat her usual Saturday lunch cooked over a single gas ring, but she didn't say so, merely joining in the general conversation and keeping as far away from Brick as she could. After lunch Cosy led her up to see her room. 'We thought you'd like one overlooking the maze,' she told her.

Emma goggled. 'Is there anything this place hasn't got?'

'Can't think of anything. Let's see.' Cosy began to tick things off on her fingers as she spoke. 'Pool, sauna, solarium, squash court, billiard-room, grass court, lake, rose garden, maze, both written up—you'll find the books in the library—twenty-seat movie theatre, plus helicopter landing-pad, and full suite of offices with fax——'

'Stop! That's enough!' Emma was smiling but, underneath, her opinion of Brick Dryden was just as critical. 'Is it all really Brick's—or is he just some sort of super-executive?'

'Don't you believe it. He started with one small timber company ten years ago. I've told you he's a serious guy. Never stops. It's all his, every last stick.'

Out of my league anyway, thought Emma, marking up yet a further objection to him. 'I thought he said he didn't own this place,' she said, remembering his somewhat cryptic remarks on her first visit here.

'That's true. You'll have to ask him if you're interested. I think he leases from some charity or other.' But Cosy wasn't interested in all that. Instead she threw open the doors of one of the wardrobes in Emma's room. 'Not a single stitch has been worn. They're only out of their wrappers because Miriam has a tidy mind.' She gave Emma a mischievous grin. 'I'm quite looking forward to seeing you in some of this stuff. It should make us perfectly indistinguishable!'

CHAPTER EIGHT

EMMA was content to have Cosy's chatter in her ears all day if it meant she was going to have a constant chaperon too. Even Brick wouldn't try anything on—surely?—while the two of them were together. She didn't, of course, give two pence for his promise not to lay a finger on her.

Together the two girls wandered about the large house and grounds, Cosy pointing out all its advantages and Emma expressing her unlimited approval. Eventually she said, 'You sound as if you're trying to sell the place to me!'

'Not the *place* exactly. . .' Cosy was watching her carefully.

Assuming she meant their way of life, her own and Brick's, Emma gave a light laugh. 'Right, I'll buy!' Then she pulled a face. 'If only! But lucky you—Brick really seems to have everything.'

Cosy furrowed her brow. 'On the surface, yes. . .' She was watching Emma again. 'But there's more to life than material things.'

Emma was surprised to hear this coming from Cosy, but she didn't say anything and Cosy herself changed the subject. 'If you've got over your tiff let's go and find him.'

Emma stiffened. 'I think I'll stay here in the sun for a while. You go. You've scarcely seen each other since he came back.'

'You're going to sit out here?' Cosy looked round at

the still bare rose garden. 'At least go on to the terrace where there are a few flowers in bloom!'

'No, it's a nice little sun-trap here.' They were by now sitting in a small arbour of clipped yew. The advantage of staying in this exact spot, she was thinking, was that Brick would never find her, tucked away like this. For the first time since meeting him outside her flat this morning she felt safe.

Cosy nodded and wandered off. 'We'll have a game of squash later,' she warned. 'I'll come and find you.'

Emma closed her eyes. Even at this time of year the sun was really warm. She must have dozed a little for it was the sound of a soft footfall on the path that woke her. When her eyes blinked open the first thing she saw was Brick's face glowering at her from over the top of the hedge. He strode into the arbour and sat down beside her.

'Cosy said you were here. What's the game?'

'I don't know what you mean,' she countered, not deigning to look at him. The hairs on the back of her neck prickled at his nearness.

'You mean you're not avoiding me?'

'No.'

'I've had more attention from a stone,' he observed drily.

'Sorry about your ego,' she riposted. 'Look here,' she turned to him, 'you promised you wouldn't bother me if——'

'My words, if my memory serves me as well as it usually does, were, "I won't lay a finger on you"—well?' he demanded. 'I'm keeping my word, aren't I?'

'Nevertheless, I wish you'd go away and leave me in peace. I just want to sit here and enjoy the sunshine while it lasts.' She closed her eyes firmly and pretended to be doing nothing but drinking in the watery beams.

'There's a solarium if you're trying to get a tan,' he informed her blandly. 'You'd have more luck there.'

'I prefer fresh air and solitude,' she told him.

He fell silent. With her eyes tight shut she couldn't be sure what he was up to. The silence lengthened. Finally she thought he must have gone, treading so quietly, like the jungle animal he was, that she had failed to hear him leave. She opened her eyes.

'Still here,' he murmured close by her left ear.

For the second time since she had met him she felt a blush ride up her body in a soft flood as she saw his dark eyes laze over her upturned face. 'No one can have everything,' she managed to say, unconsciously echoing the conversation she'd had with Cosy and firmly closing her own eyes again to shut him out.

He gave a snort. 'Certainly not as far as you're concerned. No one can have anything.'

'You'll have to be content with just the *one* of us,' she reprimanded.

'But the question is, which one?' he came back quickly.

'That's already decided,' she told him. Opening her eyes again, she said, 'I'm going in. Will you excuse me?' Before he could reply she got to her feet and hurried from the arbour. Once clear of the sweet, heady smell of evergreen and the dangerous proximity of a male unmistakably on the prowl, she felt her senses return to normal. He didn't need to lay a finger on her so long as he was going to accost her at every turn with that husky-voiced drawl. It still meant, despite his promise, that he was in single-minded pursuit.

What he had warned her when he'd issued the invitation was worth bearing in mind—there was safety

in numbers! She hurried into the house, determined
not to be caught alone again.

'There you are!' It was Cosy. 'Feel like a game of
squash now?'

'I'd like nothing better.' Slamming a ball against a
brick wall was one way of getting rid of her tensions.
She was on the point of asking Cosy why she'd told
Brick she was hidden in the arbour, but on second
thoughts saw that it would draw too much attention to
her feelings on the subject. Inevitably Cosy would start
to ask questions. And Emma couldn't trust herself to
answer without giving everything away. Her feelings
were too wild to bear public examination as yet.

'Come up. I've got sports gear in my room,' invited
Cosy.

A few minutes later both girls surveyed themselves
in the long mirror in Cosy's dressing-room. They were
dressed in identical white T-shirts and shorts, and there
was no way of telling them apart.

'It's like looking into a mirror,' said Emma, turning
to gaze wide-eyed at her double.

'Let's go down and see what reaction we get!' Cosy
was already halfway to the door.

Feeling self-conscious, Emma followed. The first
person they came across was Jon. Cosy went up to him
and in a passable imitation of Emma's accent asked,
'Coming to watch us play, Jon?'

His eyes swivelled from one to the other. 'Er. . .yes.'
He hesitated.

'Great! Let's—er—punch on down!' said Emma,
coming up.

Jon grinned. 'I couldn't tell you apart at first.' He
slipped an arm round Cosy's shoulders. 'Your accent's
a real give-away, Emma. Luckily!'

Cosy gave a hoot of laughter and shot Emma a delighted glance. 'What a rotten nuisance,' she said. 'I knew Jon would suss—guess who was who!' When they left him he was looking after them with a puzzled frown, obviously not understanding why they were giggling together like two schoolgirls.

While they played Emma was conscious of two pairs of eyes watching them from the balcony. The darker of the pair were the ones that put her off her game. In fact she and Cosy were so evenly matched it was difficult to separate one from the other. It suddenly dawned on Emma that she had found the perfect camouflage. Talk about protective colouring! Brick wouldn't dare make suggestive remarks to her so long as he was unsure which of them he was addressing!

When they came off the court she suggested they keep up the pretence for a little longer. They both showered, then at Cosy's suggestion decided to have a dip in the pool. Emma was dubious when she realised Cosy fully intended to bathe in the nude.

'You can't wear anything, Emma. They'll guess it's you!'

'I'm not skinny-dipping in front of two men I hardly know!' she exclaimed.

With a sigh Cosy found a couple of bikinis from somewhere. 'This'll have to do you,' she said. 'OK?'

Emma thought they were rather revealing, but knew it was pointless to say so. Besides, the men were having a game of squash themselves now, and with luck she could be in and out of the pool before they finished.

It was heavenly lazing about under the domed roof with the sun, warmed by the glass, dappling gently over their skin. Life at Rosedene seemed to be geared to floating in a haze of self-indulgence. 'This is a real pleasure dome,' observed Emma, swimming on her back to where Cosy was treading water.

'More pleasure to come,' murmured Cosy, glancing over towards the poolside. Emma followed her glance and gave a gasp.

It was right what Cosy had told her about Brick. She could see for herself what she had only previously suspected—he had the most perfect body of any man she had ever seen. He was slightly tanned, and his muscles bulged in all the right places from the wide, well-developed shoulders, to the span of his muscular chest and down to the arrowing flatness of his abdomen. Emma tried not to gape at the brief white swimming-trunks he had on—they left nothing to the imagination at all. Hard thighs tapered to a pair of strongly defined calves as he flexed and prepared to dive.

'Golly,' she breathed admiringly despite herself. She sank beneath the surface, her face aflame.

When she eventually came up for breath Jon was running along the edge and dived in with a splash and began to swim towards her. Before she had time to work out what had happened to Brick, Jon was beside her and grasping hold of her long hair, asking with a grin, 'OK, which one are you?'

'Guess!' she giggled, trying to swim away, but he held on to her hair until Cosy swam up, teasing,

'I'm Emma! I'm Emma! Come and get me!'

When Emma surfaced again, Jon had them both by the hair and was preparing to dunk them alternately until they admitted who was who. Then suddenly she felt hands like steel grip her round the waist. This wasn't Jon, she knew at once. As she corkscrewed within his grasp, she glimpsed Cosy swimming strongly for the edge with Jon furrowing in hot pursuit.

By now Brick had her firmly in his arms and she was swooningly conscious of the long length of his powerfully muscled body sliding intimately over her own. Her back arched in an attempt to wriggle away but he was laughing, his lips inches from her own, a confusion of waves and water and tangled limbs sending her into utter confusion.

She felt his mouth touch the side of her face, no sooner aware of it than it was somewhere else, colliding in random, spine-tingling contact as she undulated helplessly within his embrace. Somehow they were in deep water, one muscular arm tightening round her upper body, the other drawing her snaking hips hard under him in a posture of flagrant intimacy as he tried to quell her struggles. What had begun as a game instantly became something dangerous. She felt her defences crumble as his superior strength overwhelmed her.

'It's me, Emma!' she warned, gulping water as they both slid beneath the surface. When she came up again his laughing hazel eyes were only inches from her own.

'I know it's you, idiot,' he murmured. 'You're as slippery as a mermaid, keep still.' His hands slithered over her silky skin as if to force an even more complete surrender from her. 'Steady!' he growled as she wriggled even more furiously.

His thighs locked themselves round her flailing legs, one hand wrapped cobra-like round her waist, and the other one came out to grasp her by the back of the head, coiling her long hair round and round his hand until she was a prisoner and he could turn her face up to his.

'*Don't*——!' she gasped, feeling herself slide helplessly under the water as his mouth came down hungrily upon her own. Her protests were cut off as the water closed over their heads. His lips tasted of chlorine, she registered, as for a moment she surrendered to an unstoppable wave of desire, but when, still locked in an embrace, they both rose to the surface again, she took a deep, gulping breath, arching away from him with a little cry.

'Get your hands off me!' she gasped, eyes flashing a warning.

He was still smiling, his face unbearably handsome as it surfaced in front of her with little diamonds scattering from his black lashes.

'That's definitely identified Emma,' he murmured, ducking his head and swimming strongly underneath her.

Failing to guess his intention, she was taken by surprise when she felt his fingers hook inside the elastic of her bikini bottom and, bunching it in his hands, begin to drag her towards the far end of the pool. Coughing and spluttering, she tried to swivel free, nearly losing her bikini, and only managing to hang on to it with one hand, while hitting out at him with the other. Missing completely, she only splashed herself all the more in the process, continuing to lash out more furiously as he insistently dragged her along beside him.

Surfacing, he saw her hand rise to hit out again so he grabbed it, yanking it under the water so she couldn't help but swoop forward into his arms. She gave an involuntary shiver of pure pleasure as their bodies met in startling contact yet again. Now his fingers were sliding over her breasts, one hand closing possessively over the softness it found there, whipping her already tingling nerve-ends to a fever and making her nipples stand out in an unshamed reaction to his obvious desire.

His face surfaced just above her own.

'*Don't!*' she cried. '*Don't!*'

She felt his body sweep strongly over her own, the narrow hips pushing against hers, his legs binding hers again in a powerful grip that brought her under the water once more.

'What will Cosy think?' she spluttered when she rose to the surface and felt him tighten his hold round her waist. Again one hand accidentally—or was it so accidental?—skimmed her breasts.

'She's in the sauna with Jon,' he told her with a satisfied smile. 'And if she had happened to look this way she'd have assumed we'd patched up that ridiculous quarrel of ours.' He gave a soft chuckle, eyes alight with devilment.

Emma tried to twist away, but he was still intent on dragging her to the privacy at the far end.

The realisation that they were alone and she was entirely in his power sent some kind of primitive fear surging through her and she lashed out at his grinning face so unexpectedly she caught him on the side of the head.

The smile he had worn when he thought she had been playing all this time faded instantly, and when she croaked, 'You promised not to lay a finger on me, you *heel*! What do I have to *say* to make you leave me alone?' he registered blank astonishment.

Then, to her own surprise, he unlocked her from his grasp at once. The smile had gone. 'So maybe I'm only made of flesh and blood after all!' he ground out.

With a sudden surge of energy he jack-knifed away, furrowing across the pool without a single backward glance.

She watched him go leaving scarcely a ripple, the rhythmic in and out of his powerful limbs sheer poetry in motion as he did a fast crawl towards the steps.

She trod water, feeling his abrupt departure like a physical wound.

As soon as the sauna door closed behind him she climbed out. There was a lump in her throat. It was quite irrational, she told herself. There was no need to feel like this. She was shaking. It was with swallowing all that water. She wasn't used to horseplay. The memory of his body so flagrantly exploring her own under the water made her tremble just to think of it.

What on earth did he think he was up to? He was shameless. All three of them were. But life had to be a serious business for some people. They seemed to take for granted the luxury that surrounded them. She couldn't pretend everything was all light-hearted fun— him touching her like that as if he were her lover! For herself, true feeling had to be involved. She was shocked by the physical liberties he had taken. And then he had been the one to race off like that—as if *she* had offended *him*!

She decided to dress and retire from the scene altogether.

Clad in cashmere trousers and matching turtle-neck sweater in a subtle shade of oatmeal that brought out the blonde tones in her hair, just as Cosy, who had chosen the outfit, must have intended, Emma made her way down to the comparative safety of the library.

It was, she discovered, a comfortable room with several deep maroon leather armchairs in it and, as Cosy had told her, a fantastic collection of books.

She idly fingered one or two, but found she couldn't settle to anything. Her mind simply refused to stop dwelling on the subject of Brick Dryden—the way he had looked, poised on the edge like a near-naked water god ready to dive in, the way he had touched her in the underwater secrecy of the pool.

She got up and went to explore. The house seemed deserted away from the others and she roamed about, unable to remain anywhere for more than a few minutes at a time. Finally she came across one of the maids who, when she approached, told her, 'Everyone is in the sauna, miss. I've left drinks beside the pool for you all.'

Emma thanked her and walked as far as the double doors before hesitating with her hand on the knob. Dared she face Brick just yet? Or was she going to run away and prove she couldn't handle the situation as he had seemed to suggest the other evening?

With a deep breath she pulled open the doors and went in. As she sat down she reassured herself that, now she was fully clothed, Brick would be uninterested in her while Cosy flaunted her nude body at his side—for as he had just confessed, she cynically reminded herself, he was made of flesh and blood, wasn't he?

Apparently they were still in the sauna and she could hear laughter echoing from within. She chose a magazine at random from the pile provided. Then, conscious of every ebb and flow of sound from the wooden cabin, she flicked through the pages, scarcely registering a single word though her eyes never lifted from the printed page.

Brick was the first to emerge. He had a towel over one shoulder. Otherwise he was stark naked. His skin, she registered with dull shock, was pale gold with a flush of perspiration on it. It contrasted dramatically with his black hair. As soon as he noticed her he came across. She lowered her eyes at once and kept them riveted to the page.

'Fascinating magazine, is it? I didn't know you were interested in motor racing.' He was rubbing himself dry, apparently without a shred of self-consciousness. When she chanced a glance at him he was fastening the towel round his hips. Apparently satisifed that he was decent, he sprawled in one of the loungers and reached for a glass of fruit juice. 'You should have come in,' he told her. 'Just what you need to help you unwind.'

'What is, honey?' Cosy came bounding out and caught the last few words. He lifted his head and reached for her. 'You are, Cosy, baby: Just what a man needs at the end of a long, hard day.'

Emma flinched as Cosy flicked her towel at him. 'A playmate, Brick honey? That's new, coming from you!'

She draped her towel loosely around herself and soon Jon joined them. Emma noted he was the only one who emerged decently covered. She felt stuffy and self-conscious, sitting there garbed from neck to ankle in cashmere, even though it clung and flowed to every curve, but Brick's glance even with Cosy lying beside him was enough to strip her to the skin, and that, though only imagination, was enough to bear.

'We'll have a look at this footage after dinner,' he announced. 'See if you've justified yourself, Cosy. Greg will expect a report when he rings in.'

'You never rest, honey. Can't you give me a chance to recover from that ducking you gave me?'

When he left after a minute or two to go and dress, she leaned across to Emma. 'You really don't get on with him at all, do you. I *am* sorry. I thought it was something you would sort out once you were here together.'

Emma dropped the magazine to one side. 'I didn't

mean to be a killjoy just now. I just felt I'd had
enough. . .' She bit her lip. 'I've never been particu-
larly keen on swimming.'

'You mean you don't like feeling out of your depth,'
Cosy judged, patting her arm. 'He's not an easy guy
sometimes. Forgive him.'

Puzzled by this last remark, Emma watched as she
got up and went to change. Forgive him, Cosy had
said. But for what? Did Cosy know he had made
advances to her? Was she trying to tell her that she, his
fiancée, could forgive him that, and therefore, as one
of the family, Emma should too?

The viewing-room, large enough to be classed as a
small cinema, was in a part of the vast cellars not given
over to wine. Jon and Cosy were sitting side by side,
then there was a space of a chair or two, then came
Emma and then, next to her, on the end of the row,
effectively trapping her in, was Brick. He had swooped
down next to her as the lights dimmed and there had
been nothing she could do about it. She was conscious
now of every little movement as he watched the film
roll.

Since the episode in the pool he had made a point of
ignoring her. Not blatant enough to arouse comment,
but, hypersensitive as she was to every nuance of the
relationship, obvious enough to herself to cause pain.
Over dinner he had been seated opposite her and their
eyes had met once as she took her place, and after that
not at all. Good, she told herself. This is exactly what
I want. She put her unhappiness down to a perverse
reaction at getting what she wanted for a change.

When the film finished there was a prolonged silence.
Nobody said anything until Brick got to up to switch

on the lights. He stood thoughtfully by the door then suggested, 'Drink, everybody?'

'I'm sorry.' Cosy didn't move and her tone was subdued. 'I was trying, honestly, Brick——'

'It wasn't all that bad,' said Jon swiftly. 'Don't forget I'm going to be editing it next week.' Emma saw him touch the back of Cosy's hand.

'Let's have the post mortem in the library,' suggested Brick. He turned and walked out.

'He's furious, isn't he?' Cosy looked at Jon.

Emma spoke up. 'I can't see what he's got to grumble about.'

'Your bit was fine,' Cosy pointed out. 'I don't know how you did it, but that boring old guy in the museum came over really well.' She shrugged. 'You said he was boring, didn't you, Jon?'

'Emma got something out of him,' Jon said. 'Come on. Let's have a drink and hear the boss's verdict.'

When they joined Brick in the library, he was lounging against the edge of the desk in the window. His gaze seemed to pass straight through Emma as she came in.

'You'll have to tell Greg yourself.' Cosy spoke first. 'He won't believe me. Tell him I'm no good at straight stuff. He'll just have to accept it.'

Brick gave a faint smile. 'It's true your forte seems to be in a lighter vein.'

'There's no way I'm going to fit in with a serious news and current affairs outfit,' she went on. 'Hell, I don't even want to! If it weren't for Greg I would never have even tried. You do believe I tried, don't you, Brick?'

He nodded.

'I'm just sorry you've had to dash back and forth across the Atlantic on my account.' She grimaced.

'Anyway, that's that.' She seemed relieved rather than the reverse.

'I'll see what I can salvage in the editing suite,' cut in Jon. 'It's not all bad.'

'Thank you. You are a pet. Now I'm going to challenge you to a game of table tennis to restore my shredded ego!' announced Cosy. She turned to Brick before she left. 'Thanks for not flying off the handle, Brick. I really did do my best.' With a final smile she led Jon from the room.

Emma, suddenly realising she was alone and unprotected, got up to go too.

'Hold it!' He uncoiled his long legs and moved towards her. She froze, eyes widening as he came near. 'Relax. I won't make the same mistake twice,' he told her bitterly.

'What do you want?' she managed to stutter.

He gave a twisted smile and his dark eyes were strangely blank. 'What did you think of the film?'

'I think Jon's probably right—he can no doubt make it a lot sharper.'

'Are you still going to persist with this stiff-necked attitude of yours?'

'I don't know what you mean.'

'For God's sake, Emma, I'm offering you a job. At least have the grace to give it some consideration.'

She sucked in a shuddering breath. 'I don't think I could ever work with you, Brick.'

He gazed long and hard at her, his face a mask telling nothing of his thoughts. 'I see,' he said after a fractional pause, dragging out the syllables. 'Straight from the shoulder. Very well. I won't ask you again.' With an expression that would have looked bleak in any other circumstances, he turned and went from the room.

Emma stood for a full minute. Her mind teemed with might-have-beens. What was the meaning of that defeated look on his face when she had turned him down? He was used to getting his own way, that she knew. But surely it didn't hurt him to suffer a defeat once in a while? She sighed and went over to the bookcase. It was nonsense to feel there had been more behind that empty look than there was. It was just one of those things that didn't make sense.

It was midnight by the time she closed the book she had been reading. Realising how rude she had been to hide herself away like this, she went in search of the others. She found Brick at once, sitting by himself, a somewhat lonely figure in the otherwise deserted sitting-room. There was a chess-table in front of him and he appeared to be mulling over some problem it presented. He looked up when she poked her head round the door.

'Have you—have you seen the others?' she asked.

'Who?'

'Jon and Cosy, of course,' she said before she realised he had probably mistaken her for Cosy. She came right into the room so he could see her properly.

'I wouldn't disturb them if I were you.'

She walked over to the cluster of chairs in front of the fire and sat down on the other side of the table. She was wondering what on earth he could mean about not disturbing them.

'They're surely not still playing table tennis?' She glanced at the clock.

He gave a cynical smile. 'Not table tennis, no. Something a mite more adult than that, I expect.'

Emma bit her lip. She wasn't stupid, but she couldn't imagine he really meant what he seemed to mean. If so why wasn't he tearing the house apart, with Jon and Cosy in it? Without thinking she leaned forward and moved one of the pieces.

'Don't tell me you play?'

'Not very well,' she admitted. 'I used to play with Edwin. He was a county champion.'

'Come on, then. Do you want to take it from here or start again?'

'Take it from here.'

He moved one of his pieces and she forced herself to focus on the game.

An hour passed. The clock was ticking comfortably in the corner and logs crackled in the wide stone hearth. Their only interaction had been in the formal ins and outs of the game. Now it was drawing to a conclusion.

Brick lifted his head before he made his final move. 'You've given me a good run. I concede.'

'But you don't *have* to,' she murmured, then she lifted her head and she knew he hadn't been talking about the game at all. His eyes had a fixed look and they turned, coming to rest their glance on the dancing flames among the burning logs.

'I—I don't think I'll ever understand you, Brick,' she floundered. In the firelight he looked impossibly good-looking, yet there was a terrible sadness about him too. Was it because of Cosy and Jon? she wondered. Had he at last discovered he had a heart that could be broken? Had he now seen with ineluctable clarity that something serious was going on—and was tonight the night when he finally conceded to his rival and bowed to his fiancée's change of heart? Emma didn't know. She could only guess.

He got up and changed the tape, filling the room with the plangent sound of pan-pipes. The music soared and fell, tugging at Emma's heart-strings with its plaintive repetitions. Brick remained where he was, leaning against the bookcase with his head on his forearm as the music played on. He looked so infinitely sad that Emma wanted nothing more than to run to him, but with all that had built up between them, cutting them off, she dared not risk the rejection she knew was likely to follow. She watched him, heart bleeding, powerless to help.

When the tension became too much she rose quietly to her feet. 'I suppose I'd better go to bed,' she whispered. 'Goodnight, Brick. God bless.' Then she quietly left the room.

When she got upstairs she tried to make herself forget the expression in his eyes, the bleak evidence of his secret anguish, but try as she might it kept coming back.

Forcing herself to go through the complete bedtime ritual, even to the point of brushing her hair to a gloss with a hundred strokes of the brush, by the time she was ready to get into bed her mind was still full of the sight of Brick, the hurt beneath that carefully blank expression.

Pulling on the blue towelling robe provided, she hesitated for a further moment, caught indecisively between two courses of action.

She could either go to bed, turning away from him and shutting him out from her heart forever. Or she could go to him. She could put aside for a moment the fact that he was probably as much to blame for the break-up of his relationship as Cosy was herself, and she could offer him the sympathy of friendship. . .

With a jolt she knew there was only one choice for her. Soundlessly she ran barefoot across the carpet and out on to the landing. The house was broodingly silent. She reached the gallery where one or two dimmed lights still burned and automatically looked down into the hall to see if the light was still on in the sitting-room. Then she came to a trembling halt. In the darkened hall below she could make out a pale shape in a long white garment. It floated romantically around her as she crossed the hall.

It was Cosy and her purpose was obvious. In the doorway of the sitting-room stood Brick. He waited until she reached him, then with a single fluid movement he enveloped her passionately into his arms.

Emma couldn't bear to suffer the sight another moment longer. Stifling a gasp of anguish, she melted back into the shadows, and when she had recovered sufficiently she stumbled back to her room in a daze of confusion.

He must love her very much, she kept repeating to herself. He must love her very, very much in order to forgive her after she'd caused him so much heartache tonight. But then, she recalled, Cosy forgave him too, and perhaps she had suffered just as much, underneath that frivolous exterior. For a moment Emma was stunned by the strength of the love they must have for each other, a love that made them both keep coming back to try again. She climbed awkwardly into bed as if her limbs had been frozen by a great chill, then the long, empty hours began.

CHAPTER NINE

EMMA tossed and turned for another hour. She had heard the clock in the hall strike three and then the half-hour and now it was striking four. Eventually she sat up and groped for her robe. It was pointless lying here with her mind on fire. Sleep would never come. She decided to go down to the library and get a book.

Remembering, as if she would ever forget, the scene that had greeted her a couple of hours ago when she had peered over the edge of the gallery, she forced herself to make sure it was clear now. There wasn't a light to be seen nor a sound to be heard. Reassured, she felt her way down the stairs, fumbling along the wall for the light switch and, not finding it, feeling her way along the panelled wall until she came to the corridor at the bottom that would lead towards the door she wanted.

About halfway along she paused. It was spooky. Even growing accustomed to the darkness, she could still only see a black well with a faint glimmer of light from a window at the far end.

Bit by bit she groped her way along the corridor to the second door, pushing it open with a gasp of relief when her fingers closed over the light switch. It was a dimmer switch, and when she pressed it the room was filled with a soft glow, scarcely enough to allow her to read the titles on the shelves. But, before she could turn it up, she felt a jolt as someone grabbed hold of her from behind. There was a muffled exclamation and the grip softened, restraining rather than as at first attacking as it tangled in the folds of her nightgown.

'I thought you were a burglar,' breathed a male voice in her ear. 'Why the hell didn't you put the lights on?'

She gave a gasp as Brick's hands swivelled her to face him, sliding up her spine, and cupping her against his own body as if to keep her prisoner. With a sick hammering of her heart, she discovered he was clad in only a short cotton kimono that did nothing to conceal the firm male contours even now pressing hard against her. She could feel his body heat overpowering her will to pull away. In that first sudden attack he had dragged her back into the corridor, and she heard the library door slip shut behind her, cutting off the light.

In the darkness she felt the roughness of his chin against her forehead as he murmured, 'Couldn't you sleep either? All I could think was what a fool I was to let you go. I should have dragged you back to bed with me whatever your arguments.'

Emma felt her knees give way.

'Why did you leave me so soon, sweetheart?' he demanded in an urgent whisper into her hair. 'I was desperate to call you back, to hold you all night. I've waited so long to have you in my arms—but I know you've needed time. You can't realise what hell you've been putting me through. . .'

Emma felt her limbs melt as his words were accompanied by a touch that began to unravel all her tension, smoothing her knotted muscles, and for the moment stopping the words of resistance she must eventually utter.

'I missed you more than I would have thought possible when I had to go back home,' he told her in a voice hoarse with emotion. 'I couldn't put it into words because I knew you'd never believe me. I felt you wanted to keep things light——' He pressed his face abruptly against hers, lifting her on tiptoe so that he could mould her body more fully against his own.

Emma felt her limbs begin to shudder with desire. He had captured her will in a moment. It was monstrous. She couldn't fight. She felt her head sink back, revealing the white arch of her throat as he leaned over her.

She lifted her head despite the hungry kisses he was giving her and tried to look him in the face, her mouth opening, despite herself, to try to make a protest, when his lips, taking her movement as an invitation, came fiercely down over her own and for long seconds all memory of anything outside this moment was wiped from her mind.

She was breathless and confused when he momentarily lifted his head to release her lips, but as she drew a gasp of air in order to say the words that would send him away his lips found hers again and his tongue began to plunder the warm cavern of her mouth, searching deep for the treasure within and making a mockery of the last vestiges of her will to resist.

By now her token attempt to push him away had failed. His broad chest seemed impervious to her resistance, and as his hands arched her heated body against his own she felt herself become a puppet under his mastery.

But it was Cosy he wanted, wasn't it? warned a small, cold voice in the torrent of emotion that was sweeping her out of control. It was Cosy, not Emma. It was his fiancée, not her twin sister. Not Miss Frost, the girl who had accidentally come into his life only a few weeks ago. She, Emma, had no right to take what didn't belong to her. She was stealing the love that belonged to another woman.

Again her two hands bunched against the packed muscles of his chest and she felt the heat of his skin beneath her fingers as his kimono gaped. With a savage movement he gripped her hands and slid them over his muscled torso, their fingers twining loverlike as she fought to resist the purpose he was making so plain to her, but her hands acquired a life of their own beneath his touch, resistance changing to acceptance as she explored his beloved shape, and she felt them slither urgently of their own free will over the hard muscles, caressing the sinews of his body, scratching over the rough hair, moving ever more hungrily against him. His mouth enveloped her own, stopping all protest.

The only sound she could emit was a small groan of pleasure as his hands, confident her own had been taught his desire, caressed the curves beneath her nightgown, pinning her so hard against him that she felt her toes lift until he was raising her in his arms, hugging her against him while one hand briefly left its position to push open the door. Then, eyes closed in a helpless faint, she felt him carry her into the dimly lit library.

Breathlessly, dipping in his arms to the rug in front of the fire, falling, almost, in a disarray of arms and legs, she felt order briefly assert itself as he masterfully dragged her beneath him. She felt her nightdress ride up. And still his mouth stopped hers with kisses.

Alarmed now by the apparently unstoppable power of his intention, she tried to struggle against him, to free at least her mouth so she could make some resistance, but he slid both hands up the length of her body, burying them in the tangle of long hair, steadying her face between his palms as she struggled so that his lips could plunder ever more passionately her depths.

Now she was desperate, ripped apart by an unstoppable desire and by the equally hard need to bring them both to their senses. There were words that had to be spoken aloud, words that would bring this heaven she was inhabiting to a heap of dust and ashes. But she had to speak.

'Brick. . . You're forgetting my twin sister——' she managed to croak. . .

'And so should you for now,' came the reply, covering her mouth.

She tore herself free. 'But——'

'It's you I'm crazy about. From that first moment—you know it. Nothing can change that—you belong to me and my entire heart is yours. . .'

'But——' she began again.

'For heaven's sake,' he muttered feverishly, 'don't stop now. I've sorted everything out with her—she knows exactly what the score is. It's over between us—if it ever started!' He held her face between his hands. 'There is nothing between us,' he said resonantly. '*Nothing*. Understand?'

Emma wanted to ask all kinds of questions, but by now he was moving powerfully over her, mouth hard with an almost mindless hunger. She knew he was on the point of taking her, and a whimper of protest rose to her throat, changing despite herself to a cry of desire as he lowered his head to taste her peaking nipples. Still she resisted, even though it was a half-hearted attempt—for if what he said was true this couldn't be wrong. Even as she hesitated the decision was snatched from her grasp. His male strength asserted its dominance and the last shred of her resistance succumbed to a helpless longing to savour at last the fruits of love.

'Do you want me?' he rasped, poising tension-filled above her. 'Yes?'

'*Yes, yes!*' she heard herself answer in a voice ripped from deep inside, a voice of primeval longing she had never heard before. And then the world seemed to balance on a single point. It became a shimmering haze of burnished gold as he plunged at last deep into her pool of love.

When she came back to a sense of their surroundings, she was aware that he had pulled the fur rug on which they were lying round her cooling limbs and that her head, resting on his broad chest, was held there by one of his hands. From the gentle rise and fall of his ribcage she guessed he might be sleeping too. She blinked herself fully awake and lay in his arms, guiltily aware that such pleasure as she felt now was unallowed, but unable to tear herself away.

A blur of grey gauze seemed to fill the windows and she realised it was dawn already.

With painful reluctance she eventually began to lift her head little by little from where he cradled it. Almost free of its precious contact, only her hair trailed over his bulging chest. Then she froze. His eyes, shadowed by darkness, were opening and he murmured blearily, 'Cosy——' and then broke off. 'You're not going so soon, are you, darling?'

She stared at him in the half-light without speaking. Cosy, he had called her. . . *Did that mean*——? Breath jammed in her throat and she felt an icy tide sweep rapidly over her skin. Surely it couldn't be true? He didn't—couldn't—no, not that! He thought she was her twin sister!

Through the haze in which she seemed to be moving she tried to make sense of the horrible world that had unexpectedly opened up.

Did it mean that wonderful night really belonged to

someone else? Was it *Cosy* he had meant to address in this excitingly hoarse whisper? Was it *Cosy* he'd imagined while he breathed such intimacies into her ear all night?

Her first impression of that kiss she had witnessed from the gallery whisked back and the only answer that now rippled to the edges of consciousness was *yes*—yes, he had thought she was Cosy all along. And, under the spell of his touch, the hard body of the man she loved speaking to her of his desire, she had leaped to believe what she had wanted to believe.

'I'll go upstairs,' she managed to croak, her voice sounding strange, unlike her own.

'I suppose we'd better go before the maid comes in.' He held her trapped in his arms for a moment. 'You look so beautiful,' he murmured, holding her as if he wouldn't let her go. 'My Gemini twin. . .'

Emma slid rapidly to her knees and stood up. 'I'll go first. . .' she whispered, her voice unnaturally husky, an unwitting disguise she realised as she moved away. She reached the door and turned once to look back. He was already crouching to pull the rug into shape, face turned towards her, nothing but a pale, beloved blur in the ever-lightening room.

'I loved you,' she whispered, not sure whether he could hear. Then she fled, without pausing for breath until she was behind her own door, hands flattening convulsively against it as too late she reclaimed the safety of her room.

What had she done? she asked herself, thoughts spinning as she frantically paced to and fro. She had unwittingly deceived two people—her own twin sister, and the man they both loved. . . She had taken what could never belong to her, and when the truth came out three lives would be wrecked.

If she could only get away, perhaps they could pretend this had never happened? she thought. Perhaps when he learned the truth he would forgive her. Perhaps it would pass as just another night of the many he and Cosy must have shared? Perhaps no one need ever know?

Guilt like a great fog settled round her shoulders. She crawled into bed, shivering, curling up into a tight ball under the duvet. What could she do now to set things to rights?

Despite her guilt and the fear of what would happen next, she slept long and late, not waking until mid-morning. Knowing she couldn't put off forever the moment when she would have to come face to face with Brick and Cosy, she showered, dressed and eventually, with her heart in her mouth, made her way downstairs. She was conscious that her face must mirror every tiny nuance of their night of love.

A maid was crossing the hall as she descended. 'Breakfast in the morning-room, miss?'

Emma nodded, unable to bring a sound to her lips.

When she went in, it was obvious everyone else had been late in getting up too. The three of them were sitting round the table in the big bay window, the beginnings of breakfast spread before them.

'Here she is, naughty, naughty!' admonished Jon at once as she came in. She couldn't stop herself giving an involuntary shiver, thinking that by now even he seemed to know what had happened, but he went on with a grin, 'It's good to know you have a lie-in now and then, Emma. I got the impression you were one of these people who go out jogging at six every morning.'

'I can't imagine why you got that impression,' she said breathlessly, not daring to glance at either Brick or Cosy. She greeted them all generally, nerve-rackingly conscious of the eyes on her as she took her place at the table.

Cosy seemed relaxed and happy. She yawned. 'I'm real fond of this old place. I shall be sorry to go back home. Did Greg say what time he would be ringing, honey?' She was addressing Brick, and let the fingers of one hand slide along his forearm. Her ring, noticed Emma, was as prominent as ever. . .

She dragged her glance away and poured herself a cup of coffee, allowing the conversation to carry on without her. Everything appeared normal on the surface. But then it would, wouldn't it? Last night must have been simply one of many for Brick and Cosy. Brick wouldn't feel the need to comment on it and Cosy wouldn't be aware there was anything to comment on!

She was so on edge that when Brick suddenly addressed a remark to her she jumped, spilling her coffee on the cloth. Cosy rang for one of the maids.

'Jon and I want to go horse-back riding,' she told Emma. 'Feel like joining us?'

Involuntarily she looked at Brick. Cosy, intercepting the glance, gave a grin. 'Brick's feeling real mellow this morning and says he intends to stray no further than the house.'

Emma flushed. She knew why he was feeling mellow. She did all she could to avoid his glance—if he once looked into her eyes he would surely know which woman he had loved all night long.

'If you don't feel like riding,' he was saying, his eyes sweeping her flushed face, 'you ought to have another

look at the library. There may be something there to
interest you.'

She gave him a startled glance. He couldn't know
the truth already? If he had mentioned anything about
last night to Cosy she would have put him right straight
away, but then she wouldn't have greeted Emma so
amiably this morning either. In fact, Cosy was looking
positively radiant—the perfect picture of a woman in
love. Emma bit her lip and glanced at Brick again, but
his eyes were two blanks.

If he only knew how much there had been to interest
her in the library last night! she thought, stoppering
down a hysterical need to giggle. It was sheer nerves.
She bowed her head, letting her long hair conceal her
face. Her nerve-endings seemed to be screeching, taut
as bow strings. 'I can't ride anyway,' she admitted
when nobody said anything.

'That's that, then.' Cosy was already getting up.
'You don't mind if we go, do you?'

Emma smiled, a poor attempt, and hoped Cosy
wouldn't guess how flooded with guilt she was at the
feeling she had cheated her.

Then another thought spun into her head. Maybe
the reason Cosy wanted to spend the morning riding
was because Brick had already hinted at something?
She had hardly sounded as if she wanted Emma with
them despite her apparent good mood.

She turned to scrutinise Brick again as he buttered
some toast, but he was looking enigmatic and she had
no idea what he was thinking. As Cosy had said, he
seemed mellow this morning, a casual white V-necked
sweater giving him a weekend look that made his dark
handsomeness so endearing. It was the first time she'd
seen him with this rumpled, 'little boy' image—so
different from the usual air of tough authority he wore.

She noticed a crinkle of dark chest hair very slightly visible in the V of his sweater. It brought memory flooding back and she wanted to reach out to him, touch his arm where it rested on the table opposite, press her lips against his, feel that vulnerable softness turn suddenly into the hard masterfulness he had demonstrated last night. She wanted to rouse him to the same frenzy of loving he had shown then. Only the agonising knowledge that it had been meant for someone else stopped her from throwing all caution to the winds and reaching out to him. It was forbidden to touch. She mustn't give way.

'Daydreaming, Emma?' Jon's voice shattered her tortured and torturing ruminations.

'We asked what you were going to do.' Cosy smiled.

'I'll take care of Emma.' Brick regarded her steadily from the other side of the table. Cosy glanced quickly from one to the other. 'Good, that's settled, then.' She was obviously confused by the atmosphere between them as, in fact, was Emma herself.

Guilt made her jerk up her head. 'I feel like having a look at the Sunday papers and just getting away from people, actually. You go with Cosy if you like, Brick. Don't feel you have to stay behind just because of me. . . I'm sure,' she added, 'you ride as well as you do everything else.' She could have bitten off her tongue after this last remark.

Cosy was frowning. 'Sort it out between you. I'm going. Coming, Jon?'

'You bet.' They both rose and Emma leaped to her feet at the same time. She would have to confess to Cosy what had happened between herself and Brick, she couldn't deceive her own twin sister, but now wasn't the time to do it. She would wait until they were alone together. It was something she shouldn't avoid.

In the meantime the least she could do was keep away from Brick.

She followed them out of the room, talking animatedly about anything that came into her head, conscious of Brick's brooding glance following her out. She didn't know why he had had that brooding look every time she chanced to catch his eye. The predatory jungle cat and the 'little boy' look were ambiguous aspects in the character of one and the same person. He was the most confusing man she had ever come across.

When Cosy and Jon left the house, Emma followed them as far as the terrace. She had caught sight of Brick in the library through the half-open door. Armed with a sheaf of newspapers, she sat at one of the garden tables with the intention of keeping as much space between the two of them as possible.

She was still there, shivering slightly in the watery sunbeams, when, an hour later, one of the maids came out to tell her coffee was being served in the sitting-room. Knowing it would look odd if she went on shivering outside any longer, she made her way back into the house. He hadn't come to seek her out. That must mean his imagined reconciliation last night with Cosy had taken his mind off his pursuit of herself.

Some of the guilt lifted when she realised she might have unwittingly helped the two of them to patch things up.

Perhaps if she could tell Cosy the truth as soon as she came back, Brick himself—the idea shocked her— Brick need never actually know? Her mind whirled at the thought. Was it ethical? she wondered. If it helped to get the two people she loved most dearly in the world over a sticky patch in their relationship, then was it possible to justify the deception? I'm snatching at straws, she acknowledged guiltily. But what else to do without hurting anyone? The thought of prolonging the deceit warred against her natural honesty. But if it saved the relationship, came the doubting voice again, wouldn't it be for the best?

Further than that, she found herself continually shying away from what would follow when she confessed to Brick himself. Does he *have* to know? she asked herself for the hundredth time. Now the question had taken shape it battered relentlessly in her skull. Could she, should she, *dared* she confess?

Racked by first one argument and then by its opposite, her nerves were strung to breaking-point. Brick appeared from nowhere as she came in from the garden.

'Solitary creature, aren't you?' he murmured as she crossed in front of him to take a chair by itself near the window.

She looked up with as much sharpness as if he had laid a hand on her. 'Am I?' she asked dumbly, aware that her voice was unnaturally high.

Brick shrugged.

It had been a casual remark and now she was reacting as if it were some sort of inquisition. Guilt flamed through her once again. The fact of their lovemaking in the near dark careered through her thoughts, obliterating all others. Suddenly it was impossible that they could be standing on opposite sides of the room as if everything was the same as it had been before that event. How could he not know he had been her lover, in her, round her, a complete part of her, only hours ago? Why did it not show? Why did the very walls not scream the truth? Weren't even the atoms of the oxygen they both breathed alive with the knowledge of their union?

She closed her eyes, dizzying herself with the effect of forcing herself to understand.

He was beside her. A hand skimmed her shoulder, hovering as if uncertain whether to touch or not. She stepped back.

'It's all right. No need to shy away from me. I am house-trained, you know. I'm not going to ravage you here and now on the coffee-table.'

Her eyes flew to the heavy Italian marble table positioned a few feet away.

He gave a husky chortle of amusement. 'Emma, your eyes speak volumes. Don't put wicked ideas into my head. . .' Now his hand really did come down, massaging the tendons of her neck, easing imperceptibly back and forth down her spine, across the bones of her pelvis, drawing her, bit by bit—so slowly she could almost pretend it wasn't happening—into the orbit of his power again. She could feel the heat of his desire reaching out for her. It was a magnetic force. It was irresistible.

Then a maverick thought leaped into her mind. Last night he had imagined he was seducing Cosy in this lethal, masterful fashion. Melting her resistance. Dominating her will. Asserting complete control.

This morning he was doing the same thing—to another woman. What sort of man would do that? Had he no principles?

She gave a hoarse cry of protest and the words she should have spoken last night were wrenched from between her lips. 'I'm not Cosy!' she blurted, side-stepping beyond the curve of his arm. 'You know full well I'm not!'

With a jerk of her head, she flung herself across the room, and, not caring what happened to her dignity, ran as fast as she could upstairs. When she gained her room she locked the door. He mustn't come after her. Even now she knew her resistance hung by a thread.

She lay on the bed, panting with more than the physical exertion of breaking away from him. Her heart was thumping and her mouth dry. Would it ever be safe to go near him again?

CHAPTER TEN

LUNCHTIME brought a rapid knocking on her door. 'Emma, it's me! We're back!'

Emma ran to open it. 'Cosy!' She braced herself. She would tell her everything. But Cosy was halfway down the corridor already.

'I'm just going to have a quick shower. I smell horribly of horse! Brick said you were skulking up here. Come on down and have some lunch and I'll tell you about my marvellous morning!' Then, before Emma could add anything, she had disappeared into her room and shut the door.

At that moment the gong resounded from the hall announcing lunch. Obivously confessions would have to wait. In the meantime she would make the most of the next few hours for Cosy's sake, for soon she would have to tell her the truth. She dreaded the consequences—wondering if Cosy would ever want to speak to her again. After today Cosy—as well as Brick—would be on the far side of the ocean, and whether they went on as twins in their newly discovered relationship depended on what happened next.

If this was the last time they would be together Emma wanted everything to be perfect. With this resolution at the forefront of her mind, she played the perfect guest and lunch turned out to be an almost enjoyable occasion. Cosy and Jon were in high spirits after their ride and Emma responded with a streak of frivolity that almost came from the heart. Brick, she discovered without surprise, could be wickedly amusing when he chose. Only the fact that confession-time loomed cast a shadow over Emma's participation. She braced herself, but was unexpectedly forestalled yet again.

Cosy beamed round at everyone when the meal was drawing to a finish. 'Now we're all going to do what the typical Victorian house guests used to do after lunch!' She rose to her feet. 'Come on, everyone, follow me!'

Jon was already at her heels. 'No goofing off, you two, follow us. Chief's orders!' He halted when Cosy did in order to wait for them both.

Brick unfolded himself from his chair. 'Emma?' He raised his eyebrows. Feeling reassured by the presence of the other two, she followed them outside.

Cosy began to stride briskly across the lawn with everybody at her heels, and only when she reached the clipped yew hedge of the maze did Emma guess what her plan was. She took Emma by the arm and the two girls went in first. 'Count to twenty, then come and find us!' called Cosy over her shoulder to the men, pulling Emma along with her round the first turn. 'Now split!' she hissed. 'That'll really confuse them!'

Emma watched as her twin ran on ahead until she came to the first corner. Already she could hear Jon and Brick on the other side of the outer hedge. Not knowing quite which way to go, she took to her heels, making a different turn from Cosy and finding herself faced with three separate choices of avenue. Without thinking she plunged into the middle one and ran on.

'Cooee!' she heard Cosy call at intermittent intervals from behind the hedge. Answering whoops she took to be Jon in hot pursuit. The sounds seemed to come from all directions. Now near, now distant. She tried to peer through the close-cropped yew but it was an impenetrable barrier of tightly packed little leaves. She ran on until she came to an open space with a sundial in the middle. Here she paused until she caught a glimpse of Cosy running past the end of one of the lanes. Thinking to join her, she followed, but was soon in a worse state of confusion. Voices came from different directions, still near, then once again at a distance.

Of Brick she had heard nothing and wondered if he had given up, judging it too childish a pursuit for someone of his maturity. Eventually she came to a wooden seat and rested for a moment until she could work out some stratagem for finding her way back to the others. She knew she was hopelessly lost.

The voices had faded now and all she could hear was the liquid sweetness of an invisible bird in full song. A flash of something white passing the end of the avenue made her turn her head.

So Brick hadn't deserted them after all! It was too late to escape without being seen, he was already moving silently over the cropped turf towards her, but she sprang to her feet anyway and made off down the first avenue she came to. She heard him close behind her. He was in pursuit.

Pressing into a narrow gap between two hedges, she imagined she could give him the slip that way. But he was too sharp-eyed, and doubled back just as she was emerging. She spun on her heels and threw herself into the next available opening. The game was in earnest now, his doubling back and forth forcing her ever deeper into the intricate network of paths. Time and again she found herself in a blind alley and had to dart back, losing ground. He was beginning to move more slowly, confident he could take his time and she would fall into the trap herself.

With a gasp she found an avenue where she hadn't been before and ran blindly along it, hope rising that she had shaken him off at last. Breath wrenching in and out of her bursting lungs, she flew round the corner, to find its only exit blocked by her sardonically smiling pursuer.

'Right to the very heart, Emma. Well done!' He moved over the turf towards her, taking his time, a dangerous smile on his face as he announced, 'You deserve a very special prize!' He reached out, tilting her chin masterfully towards him.

'How do you know who I am?' she blurted, trying to back off.

'I know *you*. . .' He began to bend his head.

'Don't kiss me, Brick, not here, not now, not with Cosy so close at hand! I beg of you!' she breathed, scrambling her words in her haste to get them out. 'Please, Brick, not now, not here, no——'

His lips were lowering inescapably towards hers.

'Please, Brick. . .please!'

'You don't have to beg me, Emma. I'm doing this very willingly——'

'I mean please don't. . .' she said huskily, confusion reigning as his fingers slid teasingly down the side of her jaw.

His eyes became sombre. 'Why have you slipped back into the mood you were in yesterday?' he asked. 'I thought you'd managed to get over the fact that I persuaded you to follow your real wishes and come out here for the weekend? You seemed to be content with your decision to give in. . .'

She shook her head.

His fingers were stroking the silky skin of her neck, moving lower to caress her collarbone beneath the edge of her blouse, and the little extra pressure he exerted brought her one faltering pace closer. Then their bodies skimmed each other, lightly, tantalisingly, the scent of yew blossom, spring grass, and his own all-male scent of leather and soap dizzying her senses, recalling that first impression she had had when he had bestowed the first kiss, that image of wide open spaces, of a world without limit.

Now she croaked her denial of his magic despite the waves of need beginning to draw her on to destruction again.

He bent to kiss her lips with a deliberation that showed he was still in control. 'Why have you changed?' he persisted.

'I—I didn't know I had,' she blurted.

His black eyebrows raised in astonishment. 'But you're saying no to a mere kiss now, whereas last night you didn't say no to *anything*.'

'Last night?' she blurted, stunned at what he seemed to be implying.

'When I mistook you for a burglar and you revealed your true feelings at last,' he went on with a cruel smile. 'They were your true feelings, weren't they, Emma?'

So he knew! He had known all along! Her mouth opened in astonishment. He took it as an invitation to press his own mouth hotly against hers, and she felt his tongue probe excitingly, rendering her defenceless again.

When he released her his eyes still held the same question.

But she avoided it and instead asked, 'How on earth did you know?'

He smiled. 'Because of you. . .simply you.'

'I thought you'd mistaken me for Cosy. You said——' She brushed a hand over her forehead. 'How did you know?' she asked. It seemed more surprising that he did know now than that he didn't.

'You happen to wear a particular French perfume,' he told her. 'It's been driving me mad with images of you ever since you first came near me. . . It's unmistakable—and so are you. . .'

So it was true! He *had* known! But now her thoughts spun on to another tack. If he knew, had known from that first moment when he had held her in his arms, then, judging by the closeness that still existed between himself and Cosy, what he had told her last night about there being nothing between them had been false, surely? It could only mean he had knowingly deceived the woman he was going to marry, just as he had deceived her too!

She dragged her mouth from beneath his, pulling his head back as her fingers tightened in his hair. 'You're forgetting Cosy!' she threw at him. 'How could you make love to me while she's still here?' she demanded with gathering contempt.

He twisted her hands behind her back in a savage show of sudden anger, pinning them there and rasping, 'I wasn't aware it bothered *you* at the time!'

'I happened to fall for that line about there being nothing between you!' she flung back, and then she added, 'You don't realise how overwhelming you are. I couldn't help myself.' She hated admitting it but it was true. 'You forced me to give in,' she added. 'You wouldn't take no for an answer!'

He gave a scathing laugh and tightened his grip. '*Forced* you? Really?' Plainly he was trying to make her feel she had been as eager as he had been. His voice lowered menacingly. 'I suppose this is forcing you as well. . .' And he moved his lips hungrily over hers, whipping an involuntary response from her that

drove her to a further loss of control when he ran both
hands over her entire body until she was unsure where
her own limbs ended and his began. Abruptly he stilled
her undulations, once again establishing his choice in
the matter and gripping her in a steel trap, arms once
more pinned behind her back.

She began to sob. Suddenly, deeply, without
restraint. Raw breath racked through her heaving
frame. The anguish of wanting him and knowing it
could never go any further lashed her mind into a
torment. 'I hate you, Brick. You're despicable and
faithless and you knew what effect you had on me.
You played on it. You've known all along how you
make me feel. I've tried to fight it. But you played on
it deliberately! I care so much for Cosy, she's the only
relative I have in the entire world. I can't bear the
thought of hurting her. And I hate you because you're
just hateful and you're using me and deceiving her and
I should never have let you make love to me. I hate
myself as much as I hate you!'

His face seemed scarred with instant rage. 'You silly
fool! Don't ever say that again! Do you really believe I
would make love to one woman while still engaged to
another?'

His words brought her heaving sobs to an astonished
halt. Disbelief was scrawled across her features. 'But
she wears your *ring*! Do you think I don't know that!'

'Yes. . .' His eyes darkened. 'That's true. She wears
a ring I gave her.' Hands trembling, he began to release
her from their trap. But he still held her against him.
She could feel the vibrations of his body as it throbbed
with tension. With a muffled groan he buried his face
in her hair. It was a perverse joy to know that whatever
anguish he was going through he was at least in her
arms, however briefly.

He lifted his head and for a moment she was convinced of his sincerity. She could plainly see the expression in his eyes. But even before he spoke she knew he was going to ask her to believe something he knew she would find difficult to accept.

'I can't explain in full,' he began roughly. 'Things are not what they seem between Cosy and myself. Trust me, Emma. I wouldn't lie to you. Believe one thing, there will be no marriage for the two of us. Can you accept that?'

Emma gazed and gazed into the tawny depths, a longing to take his words on trust working deep within her. But it was too difficult to accept all at once.

'Why. . .?' she probed, uncertainty clouding her eyes. 'Why say you're not engaged to be married when she plainly wears your ring for everybody to see?' She sighed, more than half convinced by the expression on his face and wanting with all her being to believe in him.

'I can't go into it right now,' he told her brusquely. 'You'll have to trust me.'

Her skin flushed as she realised he was caressing her breasts and, contrary to the doubt with which she still regarded him, her nipples were hardening with the unabashed desire to accept whatever he wanted to bestow.

She broke away, one hand clutching the front of her blouse. 'I almost do believe you, Brick. You seem to take my common sense and—and turn it into nothing. . . I can't. . . I'll have to—— Give me a little time to get used to the idea. . .' She ran a hand over her face. 'Perhaps when Cosy bears you out——?'

'I'd rather you found it in your heart to trust me without having to ask for corroboration from anyone else,' he remarked acidly. 'Surely you've been able to tell I'm sincere towards you?'

She bit her lip. Had she been able to tell? Slowly she shook her head. She couldn't lie about a thing like that. She had doubted him. Did doubt him. Her eyes told eloquently of her feelings now.

He turned away with a clenching of his jaw. 'I see.' He walked to the entrance of the first avenue then turned to look back at her. 'It would have been a test, wouldn't it? How foolish of me to expect you to pass. Why *should* you trust me? You can't even trust *yourself*!' He made as if to leave her, but she called out.

'Don't leave me! I'm lost!' She meant in more ways than one.

All around them the hedges of silent yew closed in. The afternoon was already drawing to a close, dark clouds visible over the tops of the branches. He waited at the beginning of the path and when she stood beside him he reached out for her hand. 'Woman of little faith,' his lips twisted, 'let me take your hand and guide you through the maze. . .'

They were back at the exit after only one false turn. They hadn't spoke to each other, but now she said, 'How did you know which way to go?' A note of grudging admiration was in her voice.

'I read the books in my own library. There's a rather good one on the history of the house, including mazes and what they mean,' he told her. 'You know it's a sort of fanciful version of the maze of King Minos, don't you?'

She shook her head.

'But you know the legend?'

This time she nodded. 'Ariadne, daughter of King

Minos, falls in love with Theseus and leads him safely to the treasure guarded by the minotaur at its heart.'

'No minotaurs in this one, only a doubting woman by the name of Emma Andrews,' he observed drily.

'I know the rest of the story too,' she went on, matching his tone. 'Ariadne has to escape her father's wrath, so she sails away with Theseus. He, of course,' here she couldn't help giving him a quick glance, 'quickly tires of her and abandons her on the island of Naxos. So much,' she concluded, 'for the faithful lover.'

'Emma,' his voice was deep with emotion, 'don't judge me. I'm not able to speak out just yet. And I have to ask you to trust me. I want you to say you do. Love,' he went on, 'isn't any good unless it's based on trust.'

With his hands on either shoulder, she was forced to look straight into his eyes. Her own widened as if to encompass the truth. 'Yes,' she said at last, feeling she were throwing herself over the brink of a cliff, 'yes. . . I think I do trust you.'

CHAPTER ELEVEN

EVENING had come when they eventually turned towards the house. It was a blaze of light shining out of the darkness. Cosy and Jon seemed to have disappeared and Brick had shown Emma the grounds with the lake, the summer-house, the bare rose garden, and the beech copse on the other side of a small meadow which in spring, he told her, was ankle-deep in wild flowers.

And they had talked. Emma had shelved her niggling doubts and given herself up to the delight of talking to this man. Cosy had said he was clued up, and he was. There seemed to be nothing his agile mind hadn't encompassed, no book he hadn't read, no area of knowledge with which he was unfamiliar. She knew she was happy with him and could be so for the rest of her life. He seemed to take it for granted they would be together for a long time to come.

He was holding her against him as they strolled across the terrace towards the garden door, and she trembled with anticipation at what would inevitably lie ahead later that night. Before going in he kissed her slowly, deeply, almost reverently on the lips. How could I have ever doubted him? she asked herself. He held the door and she stepped inside.

Miriam was accompanied by two maids and there was an unusual air of disorder as the housekeeper hurried down the corridor towards them. 'Mr Dryden, sir, we've had the search parties out for you! Oh, I'm so sorry! We didn't know where to find you.'

'What is it, Miriam?' Brick was all alertness at once.

'It's Miss Cosy's father, sir. When he didn't ring, Miss Cosy herself put a call through. He's been taken back to the hospital, sir. An emergency, they said. She was distraught, sir. We sent out to find you at once but you were nowhere to be found.'

'So where is Cosy now?' he asked.

'Gone, sir. She and Mr Roe have driven to the airport. She was saying something about trying to get standbys for the next flight home.'

'Hell!' Brick ran a hand through his hair. 'I ought to have been found!' He remembered Emma then, and shot her a glance. 'Maybe we've been somewhat elusive for the last couple of hours. . . Not your fault, Miriam. I'm sure you did your best. Which airport have they gone to? Heathrow?'

Miriam nodded. 'She said she'd ring and let you know what's happening when they get there.'

Brick nodded. After she'd left them he turned to Emma. 'If she manages to get me a ticket I think I may have to leave with them.' He pulled her into his arms. 'Let's hope it's not going to be for long.' His mouth pressured the side of her head and they clung together, not speaking. There was a polite cough. It was one of the maids.

'Telephone, sir. Miss Cosy on the line.'

Reluctantly Brick released Emma and followed the maid into the study. When he emerged a few minutes later his face was grim. 'They've got me a ticket. I'll have to go. It sounds bad. He had a stroke late yesterday.' He came to stand over her. 'They've taken my car and I'm going to have to go over in the limo. I'll send it back for you. Burt'll drive you to work

tomorrow morning. You'll have to leave early
though. . .' He held her hands tightly between his own.
'There's scarcely time to tell you how much I love you.
It's going to be touch and go whether I make the flight
on time. . . Take care, sweetheart. I hate to think I'm
going to be spending the night thirty thousand feet up
in a tin box. . .instead of in bed—in heaven—with
you!'

Emma felt bereft after she saw the black limousine
carry him away. The house seemed enormous, empty,
like a mausoleum. She walked beneath the echoing
glass dome of the swimming-pool, remembering how
he had looked yesterday, all bronzed and athletic,
poetry in motion as he'd ploughed through the turquoise water, crystal drops spraying from his dark
lashes as he'd emerged beside her.

She was just crossing the hall to the sitting-room with
the idea of simply curling up in front of the television
when one of the maids saw her. 'Miss,' she asked,
'should I continue packing Miss Cosy's things ready to
send over to Canada? I don't like to think of that dress
being crushed up for longer than necessary.'

'I don't suppose she'll want you to send anything all
that way, will she?' Emma raised her eyebrows.

'Definitely the dress,' said the maid. 'She was going
to take it back with her tomorrow before all this upset
came about. But she left in such a hurry she forgot
about it.'

'Is it a special dress?' asked Emma. Cosy hadn't
mentioned anything to her.

She followed the maid upstairs, wondering if there
was anything she could do to help. The girl went over
to a large carton on the bed. 'I was wondering if I
ought to take it out and hang it up until she lets us

know how to send it on?' As she spoke she lifted the lid and carefully removed several layers of tissue paper before drawing forth a delicate froth of white lace, its long, ruched skirts sewn with tiny seed-pearls, and of such ethereal and unmistakably bridal appearance that Emma could only gasp. She gazed dizzily at the delicate confection of silk and ribbon-lace as it was laid carefully on the bed.

'She's going to be a gorgeous bride, isn't she?' breathed the maid, oblivious to the chaos of Emma's feelings. 'But this poor dress. First it was in its box then it was hanging up then it was in its box again. Now I suppose I'd better hang it up yet again!' She glanced at Emma for confirmation. 'Are you all right, miss?'

Emma nodded weakly. He had lied to her. He had stated that there would be no marriage. Now she was staring at the dress Cosy was going to wear on her wedding-day.

She turned with a choking feeling and reeled to the door. 'Hang it up until someone gives you further instructions,' she advised over her shoulder. She didn't know which way to turn. He had lied to her. He had asked her to trust him. And all the time he was lying.

The next few days passed in a hell of despair. Anger at how he had deceived her, shame at the way she herself had deceived Cosy, recriminations at the gullible way she had believed every lying word he had uttered vied for attention. She was glad she had work to do and threw herself into it like a maniac, not caring that the quicker she finished, the sooner she would be out of a job. The future stretched ahead like a desert. She couldn't imagine caring about anything or anyone ever again.

When she arrived at Lady Burley's in the limousine

that black Monday morning she had warned Jack not to put any calls through to her. Back at the flat there was a permanent note on her door: 'Do not disturb'. The phone did ring. It rang at work and at home. Judy picked it up one morning and told her it had been a man's voice. 'Your Canadian cowboy,' she joked. Emma had been unable to tell her how the affair—for that was all it had been—had collapsed.

One of these days she would be able to talk, but not yet.

He rang her at work too. Jack was puzzled. 'It's him again,' he told her.

'Tough,' she replied succinctly, not looking up from her notes.

As one week became two and the second melted into the third she felt she was learning to hold back the tide—the black waves would not sweep her under. She would fight them to the end.

Then her thoughts began to dwell on Cosy, on the man who was her twin's adoptive father whose illness had precipitated the whole débâcle. Had he succumbed to his illness? Was Cosy at this moment in mourning for the man who had chosen her from out of all the other babies at the orphanage so long ago? How must she feel? Was she as bereft as Emma herself, albeit for a different reason?

Her hand hovered over the phone and she longed to ring her twin. She knew Cosy had tried to contact her. Messages had been left, asking her to get in touch.

One day she decided she simply had to ring her. Why should she let that man come between her and her twin sister? It wasn't right. They had been torn apart almost at birth, and now they had found each other it would be a double tragedy if they were parted again.

She dialled the number on the card Cosy had first given her. An unfamiliar voice answered and then she was through.

'Emma! At last! I was so worried about you. I couldn't imagine what had happened to you. Have you been away? Where are you? How's London? When are you coming over?' Bubbling over with happiness, Cosy fired off her questions without waiting for answers. Emma wondered if the reason for her obvious gaiety was far to find. She answered all Cosy's questions and asked after Greg, relieved to hear that he had pulled through yet again.

'Wait, he's here now and insists on having a word!'

There was a pause, then a man's deep bass came over the line. 'Hey, Emma? What are you playing at? When are you going to get yourself out here where you belong? We're all waiting for you. Cosy's pining without an accomplice and she's got a lot of plans lined up for you both, so what about it?'

Emma managed to reply somehow. Everyone sounded so happy. She could almost convince herself that to be part of that happy household would ease her broken heart. But she knew that at the centre of it all was the man who was the cause of her torment.

Greg was still trying to persuade her to go over. 'I'm going to send a one-way ticket, Emma. I want you to use it. And hey, listen, you have the perfect excuse— Cosy tells me she wants you as bridesmaid at the wedding. So come on, honey. Say yes. You've got to.'

Emma gripped the phone tightly and somehow or other managed to struggle through the next few minutes. When she finally replaced the receiver she found herself trembling from head to foot even though his name hadn't been mentioned.

Why had she almost allowed herself to be persuaded? She knew she couldn't face him yet. And to see him actually walk down the aisle with Cosy on his arm. . .'*no*!' she gasped. 'I can't do it!'

It was later, when Greg's warmth and Cosy's obvious concern for her came to mind, she began to wonder if she was being spineless. Whether Brick had confessed to Cosy or not about his infidelity she knew Cosy must have him worked out by now and would know what she was taking on. More, she knew the bond between her and her twin sister was a strong one. Could she turn away from her on what was going to be the happiest day of her life?

When Greg kept his promise and an airline ticket on Concorde arrived with a further first-class ticket on a domestic flight between Toronto and Vancouver, she knew she had to shelve her personal feelings and go over. Her work here was at an end. A new life could open out for her. She would accept Greg's generous offer and once over there, when the wedding and all other obligations were done, she would take a Greyhound to Los Angeles or somewhere—lose herself in the crowds that flocked West seeking fame and fortune, never to be heard of again. . .

She outlined her intention to Judy.

'I told you there was a marriage in your stars,' she replied. 'But for some reason I had a feeling it was going to be yours.'

Emma shook her head. It was strange how she had almost been brought to the point under Brick's fatal persuasion of believing that marriage would be no bad thing after all. Well, she had learned her lesson there.

Cosy was instantly noticeable behind the barrier in the arrivals lounge at Vancouver airport. She waved as if barely able to contain her impatience while Emma waited for her luggage to come round on the carousel. Then, after Emma hoisted her one bag on to her shoulder and went to meet her, Cosy rushed forward to give her a hug. Almost at once she found herself being enveloped in another hug—this time from the powerful, white-haired bear of a man who stood beside her twin.

'Welcome home, Emma. It's a great moment for all of us,' he told her. Tears of some deep, unnameable emotion welled in the corners of her eyes and she was glad the two of them whisked her out to the waiting car at once. There was a pleasant drive to follow, crossing the Fraser River on the freeway until soon they were climbing a winding road into the mountains. Not much later they were pulling into the drive of a vast timbered house set amid massive pines.

Emma knew that Brick's name would have to be mentioned, but she put the moment off for as long as possible, leaving it to Cosy to make the opening move. When she did so, however, it was only to say that he was at his cabin in the mountains and would turn up some time. 'He's spending a lot of time up there these days. Skiing, I suppose. And plotting the further expansion of his empire, no doubt!'

Nothing more was said. Emma found a couple of rooms had been prepared for her exclusive use, and from the way everyone was talking she knew they expected her stay here to be a permanent one.

The wedding, she learned, was set for the following week. It was to be a grand affair with all of West Coast society present.

'Wouldn't it have been a lark to have had a double wedding!' exclaimed Cosy, innocently pressing the dart of sorrow even deeper into Emma's heart. 'The pastor wouldn't have had a clue whether he'd married the right bride to the right man!'

'Probably the grooms would have had a few doubts too,' quipped Emma in an attempt to lighten up.

Cosy went off to have a manicure, and, having refused on a plea of tiredness after her flight, Emma stayed behind, eventually going down to chat to Greg. Almost at once his doctor arrived and he had to leave her. 'This is your home now, Emma,' he assured her before he went upstairs. 'Feel free. We all want you here very much.'

She stood by the window looking out across the wide lawns with the mountains beyond. It was very beautiful. A rugged country with lots of space. It was very much Brick's sort of place. She remembered his expression when he had straddled one of the delicate eighteenth-century drawing-room chairs at Rosedene and she had automatically given him that look of reproof! But, tough and rugged though he was, there had also been another side to him and she remembered their conversation in the manor gardens. In the dream time. When for a short time she had lived the dream he had spun for her.

A door opened and she turned. Luckily the man just entering was more concerned with unzipping a red and white ski jacket than with looking at the room's occupant. It gave her a chance to compose herself. She was sitting on the window-seat when he looked up, the jacket trailing from one hand.

'Oh, hi. It's you.' He stomped across the room, throwing the jacket over the back of a chair and slumping down in the deep rocker by the window. She could see the top of his head over the leather back.

'Be an angel and get me a drink, would you? I've had a hell of a drive. Got a flat in the new snow Jeep and the jack froze so I thought I'd call in here first for a little tender, loving care.'

Like an automaton she went over to the drinks cabinet and searched around in it. What did he drink? She couldn't even ask a simple question like that. Despite everything his appearance had knocked her sideways. He could do anything, love a hundred other women and lie to her about it. She would still feel this stupid, irrational, wholly pointless craving for him.

She steadied her hand so that the ice wouldn't rattle against the sides of the glass to show how he was affecting her, and went over to put it on the table in front of him. He picked it up without looking at her and threw it back. 'Thank you, honey. And don't say I'm drinking too much. I've heard it all before,' he growled.

He lay back with his eyes shut. 'What day is it? I feel as if I've been out of it for weeks. Been doing too much thinking,' he went on. 'Always the same thing going round and round in my head.' He paused. Before Emma could interrupt he went on, 'There's something I never told you, though I know you guessed straight away. I was really crazy about her from the moment we first talked. . .' He paused, adding, 'Still am—you know that. Even now when it's over.' He gave a bitter laugh.

'Nothing I ever do will make me forget her. Sitting up there in the cabin I tried to work out how I was going to behave towards her when we met again. I don't know what I'm going to say when I come face to face with her. . . I might kidnap her. Take her into the mountains and never let her go.' Another laugh, full of self-mockery, was torn from him.

'You shouldn't have asked her over,' he went on rapidly. 'I might have to skip the wedding. Standing there in church next to her when——when it could all have been so different.' He got up, shooting her a swift glance as he went over to refill his glass. So far she had been too stunned to speak. He thought she was Cosy. So who was this other woman he was in love with if it wasn't his fiancée? And why was he saying all this only a week before he married?

'I know you're finding it difficult to believe that your old Uncle Brick feels like this about anybody,' he was saying ruminatively. 'Remember what you used to call me when you were a gap-toothed ten-year-old? Uncle Brick. Because I was the strong one. The one who sorted out your problems. Well, sweetheart, it's me who has the problems now. How the hell am I going to go on without her?' He turned to look straight at her.

She saw the lines of strain on his face. He was more haggard than when she had last seen him. As if he had had many sleepless nights. It added to rather than detracted from his looks. He would always be good-looking, she thought. Even when as now he was suffering. Who was this woman who had stolen his heart? Was *she* the reason he had found it difficult to be faithful to Cosy?

He came over to stand at the far end of the large picture window and gazed across at the mountains. 'We've always been such friends, you and I. Even when you went through that phase of thinking I needed a wife and generously offered yourself! I'll never forget Greg's face when you told him! And we didn't have the heart to tell him he was jumping the gun. Actually at the time it seemed like a good idea. We'd both have been free to go our own way. No questions asked. The perfect arrangement! Then you spoilt things by falling in love. . .'

He downed his drink and made as if to get another,

but apparently thought better of it and instead stood there, jiggling the empty glass in his hand.

'Greg's an old devil. If he hadn't thought he was at death's door and you were going to be stranded all alone in the wide, cruel world we'd have probably both backed out of it a lot sooner.' He laughed softly, bitterly. 'It would have made a hell of a difference to my life if we had done. Not that I'm blaming you. It took me a while to realise you were having second thoughts. For some time I imagined I was going to let two people down if I backed out. Then Greg started to get things organised from his sick-bed! The old devil must have suspected we were having cold feet! He fancied he'd make it impossible for either of us to back out, tying up the stock like that. . .'

He turned to her. 'Me, in love! It must be the joke of the century. They say those who fall last fall hardest. I couldn't believe it when I first met her. Like you, but from that first moment so unlike you. Your fabulous looks—and that mysterious something else——'

Emma gave a start of amazement and he noticed at once. Her looks, he had said. But he thought he was talking to Cosy!

There was a pause, then he went on, 'I've had to keep away from this place over the last few weeks because, hell, can you imagine what it's like to see her double around and know it's not her?'

He moved to stand beside her and Emma felt herself respond. The honey had started to flow in her frozen veins again. She looked into his eyes, his brooding tawny eyes. She saw them enlarge as if trying to take something in.

When he spoke his voice was rough. 'Hell, Cosy, don't look at me like that. I think I'm going mad. You seem——' He jerked back with a rough gesture as if to dismiss her. Emma put out a hand. She couldn't believe he was real. That they were standing here together. So near—and yet at the moment so far.

He said rapidly, 'She was everything I wanted. The sort of woman I didn't know existed. She reads, she thinks, she likes music, she's even a chess ace——'

'I think, Brick, I think. . .' she faltered, forcing the words into her mouth at last. 'I think the phrase is chess master—or maybe. . .mistress?' She moved closer, her eyes locked on his.

He moved almost imperceptibly until he was only inches from her. His face registered shock. She put out a hand.

He held it in a sudden convulsive grip. She saw his eyes lighten, dark turn to gold. '*Emma*. . .? *Is* it. . .?' He leaned into her, then with sudden savagery he drew her into his embrace, lips searching for hers, mouth hot, seeking hungrily, at first questioningly, then tongue probing full of conviction deep, deeper, into her own.

'No doubt, no doubt now,' he repeated hoarsely when he lifted his head. 'It *is* you, my precious love, my sweet Emma. I would know your mouth, your lips, your essence, in hell or heaven. . .'

Emma tilted back her head as he took her more firmly into his embrace. Gone was the broken man of a few moments ago and back was her darling, her masterful Brick. . .her love. . .her man.

It was Greg who, a few moments later, exploded into the sitting-room with the words, 'What do you know? A clean bill of health!' But the words died on his lips. 'Hold on. Isn't that the wrong man, Cosy?' Then he laughed as she turned, Brick's arms still holding her close.

'Emma! Sorry, honey, I forgot for a minute!' He looked from one to the other. 'Now don't tell me. . .?'

'We've a lot of ground to go over, Greg.' Brick glanced at Emma. 'You might have to face two brides leaving the premises next week. Think you can cope?' He moved forward. 'Maybe you'd better sit down, old man?'

Just then Cosy came in. 'Everyone's looking very strange, what's been going on?' she said at once.

'Cosy, my sweet. There's a moment when discretion is a great virtue. Brick, I'll forgive that remark about old men.' Smiling, Greg led Cosy from the room and closed the door. Brick turned at once to Emma. 'Well? What do you say? Will you give it another try?'

She allowed him to lace her in his arms. 'Yes, Brick, my love,' she answered simply. 'Yes, I will.'

He stroked her hair and said, 'We need to straighten out a few things first, don't we? But I warn you—if your answer's "no" I won't accept it without a fight.'

He pulled her down on to his knee in the deep leather armchair by the window. He was still smoothing her long hair and touching her lightly and carefully as if afraid she would vanish in a puff of smoke if he handled her too roughly. 'You do care just a little, don't you, honey? Tell me the truth, Emma, don't try to spare my feelings if you don't feel the same way.' He gave an awkward laugh. 'I've really laid myself on the line with that talk just now. It never occurred to me you'd be here already—and by yourself too.'

'I love you,' she told him again. 'I told you I did that night we made love. . .' Her mind went back to that blurted confession as she had left the library in the dawn light.

'I thought that was what you said, but next morning you were so withdrawn. Almost hostile. I began to feel you'd regretted it. That maybe your feelings weren't as strong as they seemed.'

'I was so unhappy that night we played chess,' she told him. 'I loved you so much but you didn't seem to know or care. It was horrible. I was convinced you and Cosy were going to get married, even though whenever you mentioned the word engagement you were so dismissive as if—well, I thought because you felt it spoiled your chances with other women or something.'

He gave her a scathing glance. 'So that's what you thought of me!'

'Not any longer,' she said hurriedly, and she hesitated before she went on. 'When I left you that evening to go up to bed—you were looking so unhappy I thought it was because you'd finally realised that Cosy and Jon were getting together. I thought you were hurt. I thought your suspicions had been building up and that's why you'd been ringing me from Canada the first time you left—hoping to find out whether it was true or not.'

'Cosy and I have been brother and sister for too long to have any romantic illusions about each other. And if you haven't already realised it we're very different people. I'm too serious for her, and she's too light-headed for me. I knew she was mad about Jon but they were always arguing. I fully expected him to walk out on her. Only after I learned they had taken off for Paris together—that time Cosy disappeared—only then did I guess they might make it.'

Emma remembered how Cosy had said she didn't want to be tied down, even when her feelings were one hundred per cent involved, and how she had thought she was referring to Brick—now she knew she'd meant Jon all along. 'I thought you were trying to cover up how you felt,' she told him. 'I wanted to comfort you.

But I didn't know how. That night it seemed as if you were really suffering over her. I went up to bed. But once there I felt I couldn't simply leave you by yourself. . . I decided to come back down and say something to you—just to let you know there was somebody who cared for you, somebody who would listen.' She gave him a darting glance. 'I couldn't bear to see you so unhappy.'

'You should have seen me an hour ago,' he growled. 'But go on. Why didn't you come down and avoid the hell of these last few weeks?'

'But I did!' she exclaimed. 'And the terrible thing is as I was about to come down I happened to look over the balcony—and I saw Cosy in your arms. I thought it meant you were making up. She'd said something about forgiving you. I went back to bed. But how could I sleep. . .? I mean, it was like being in hell. I wanted you both to be happy, but from my point of view. . .' She held on to him, the sudden remembrance of how she had felt that night sweeping over her.

'And that's what was in your mind when you came down again later——?' He held her close.

'I came down to get a book. . .' she butted in. 'And then you—you. . .'

'My beautiful burglar,' he murmured. 'Cosy simply came down to kiss me goodnight. She was radiant that night. Jon had finally persuaded her to clear things with Greg—tell him we had never been serious about marrying. We decided then we'd better cope with him together. We agreed we couldn't tell anyone, not until we'd put Greg himself in the picture. Then a proper announcement could be made.'

He tried to explain. 'If the Press had got wind of the fact that we'd split it would have been exaggerated to look as if Dryden was ditching van Osterbrook. The investors would have withdrawn their money faster than rats leaving a sinking ship and he would have been in a worse position than he already thought he was. Actually he's not in such dire straits after all. It's only the television company that's been on the skids, mainly because he's simply not interested enough to run it properly. It was all rather confused by the fact that he was out of action for so long. . .'

He ran a hand over her legs and said, 'I wanted to tell you properly, but events seemed to take over that night. Before I knew it we were lovers—everything seemed perfect. I thought all your doubts were over. Then next morning——'

'You called me Cosy,' she reminded. 'At least, that's what I thought you said. . .'

'When I woke up, you mean?'

She nodded.

'What I'd meant to say,' he explained, 'was "Cosy and I have never been lovers"—and then somehow it seemed too much to launch into all that at that precise moment—it was simply enough to be lying there with you in my arms at last. But then you got up. You left. Next morning my Gemini girl had become Miss Frost again.' His lips were very close to hers now and he said, 'Enough of all that. . .why didn't you see how much I loved you—especially after that beautiful night we shared? You don't imagine I make love like that with all our female guests at Rosedene, did you?'

'I did wonder. . . I supposed it must always be like that for you——'

'Like *that*?' His voice had dropped an interval. 'That volcano of wild passion? It swept me totally out of control.' He ran his lips along her jaw until they reached the corner of her mouth and stayed there. 'It was as perfect as I knew it would be. . . I could scarcely allow you out of my arms. When you suggested leaving and going upstairs I hoped you'd be wicked enough to go to my room!' He frowned. 'You were hell next morning. Angry. Nervy. Downright aggressive. I thought, Hold on, Dryden, you've blown it. But I couldn't imagine what I'd done wrong.'

'It was because I suddenly thought you'd believed I was Cosy. . . I felt terrible, so ashamed and guilty, utterly destroyed. But I simply couldn't have stopped you. . .'

'So you told me that afternoon when I trapped you in the maze.' His eyes began to gleam. 'Is this a common failing of yours, Miss Frost—this inability to say no?'

'Only with a man called Brick Dryden, sir.'

'I see.' He began to unbutton her blouse. 'I'm not sure I believe you. But I have a little log cabin in the woods,' he told her conversationally. 'It's ideal for people with your difficulty—being the sort of place where you needn't get dressed for days on end. . . I think you may need a spell up there where I can check out this weakness of yours in peace and quiet. But before I carry you off—there is one thing more.'

'What's that, my darling captor? Ask anything you like.'

'It's this. Why, after our walk and our long talk by the lake when everything seemed so perfect—why, after all *that*, have you refused all my calls since?'

She rested her face in the crook of his shoulder, drinking in the scent of him, her limbs trembling as the black days and the nights of the last three weeks came back. 'After you'd gone I saw the dress. Cosy's wedding dress,' she told him. 'It seemed to make a lie of everything you told me in the maze. I'd trusted you. I really had. Even though I couldn't work it all out, when you asked me to trust you, I did. The existence of a wedding dress seemed to invalidate everything you said.'

'My poor angel. My poor, poor angel. . . If I'd only been there to explain.' He held her very close and his voice deepened. 'You trust me now, don't you, Emma?'

'Completely.'

'And forever?'

'Forever.'

'Then is there any reason why you won't marry me next week?'

She shook her head. 'Try as I might, I can't think of a single valid reason.'

'I love you. You're as dear to me as life itself.' Their lips met.

As Brick had warned Greg, there were two brides that day a week later. Two identical faces, two identical wedding gowns, yet four hearts beating with happiness. There was no doubt in Brick's mind which was his own dear love. And in Emma's heart there was no doubt either. She glanced lovingly at the new family she had gained—a twin sister, a brother-in-law, and a father in everything but name—and then she looked lovingly at the new husband by her side. Her happiness was complete.

As they stood on the steps of the church in the spring sunshine, he bent to kiss her lips, murmuring as he did so, 'Forever mine, forever yours, forever more—twin of my heart. . .'

Harlequin Presents®

Coming Next Month

Available in July wherever paperback books are sold, or through Harlequin Reader Service:

In the U.S.
P.O. Box 1397
Buffalo, NY
14240-1397

In Canada
P.O. Box 603
Fort Erie, Ontario
L2A 5X3

OVER THE YEARS, TELEVISION HAS BROUGHT
THE LIVES AND LOVES OF MANY CHARACTERS INTO
YOUR HOMES. NOW HARLEQUIN INTRODUCES YOU
TO THE TOWN AND PEOPLE OF

One small town—twelve terrific love stories.

GREAT READING...GREAT SAVINGS...
AND A FABULOUS FREE GIFT!

Each book set in Tyler is a self-contained love story; together, the
twelve novels stitch the fabric of the community.

By collecting proofs-of-purchase found in each Tyler book, you can
receive a fabulous gift, ABSOLUTELY FREE! And use our special
Tyler coupons to save on your next TYLER book purchase.

Join us for the fifth TYLER book,
BLAZING STAR by Suzanne Ellison, available in July.

Is there really a murder cover-up?
Will Brick and Karen overcome differences and find true love?

"GET AWAY FROM IT ALL" SWEEPSTAKES

HERE'S HOW THE SWEEPSTAKES WORKS

NO PURCHASE NECESSARY

To enter each drawing, complete the appropriate Official Entry Form or a 3" by 5" index card by hand-printing your name, address and phone number and the trip destination that the entry is being submitted for (i.e., Caneel Bay, Canyon Ranch or London and the English Countryside) and mailing it to: Get Away From It All Sweepstakes, P.O. Box 1397, Buffalo, New York 14269-1397.

No responsibility is assumed for lost, late or misdirected mail. Entries must be sent separately with first class postage affixed, and be received by: 4/15/92 for the Caneel Bay Vacation Drawing, 5/15/92 for the Canyon Ranch Vacation Drawing and 6/15/92 for the London and the English Countryside Vacation Drawing. Sweepstakes is open to residents of the U.S. (except Puerto Rico) and Canada, 21 years of age or older as of 5/31/92.

For complete rules send a self-addressed, stamped (WA residents need not affix return postage) envelope to: Get Away From It All Sweepstakes, P.O. Box 4892, Blair, NE 68009.

© 1992 HARLEQUIN ENTERPRISES LTD.

SWP-RLS

- -

"GET AWAY FROM IT ALL" SWEEPSTAKES

HERE'S HOW THE SWEEPSTAKES WORKS

NO PURCHASE NECESSARY

To enter each drawing, complete the appropriate Official Entry Form or a 3" by 5" index card by hand-printing your name, address and phone number and the trip destination that the entry is being submitted for (i.e., Caneel Bay, Canyon Ranch or London and the English Countryside) and mailing it to: Get Away From It All Sweepstakes, P.O. Box 1397, Buffalo, New York 14269-1397.

No responsibility is assumed for lost, late or misdirected mail. Entries must be sent separately with first class postage affixed, and be received by: 4/15/92 for the Caneel Bay Vacation Drawing, 5/15/92 for the Canyon Ranch Vacation Drawing and 6/15/92 for the London and the English Countryside Vacation Drawing. Sweepstakes is open to residents of the U.S. (except Puerto Rico) and Canada, 21 years of age or older as of 5/31/92.

For complete rules send a self-addressed, stamped (WA residents need not affix return postage) envelope to: Get Away From It All Sweepstakes, P.O. Box 4892, Blair, NE 68009.

© 1992 HARLEQUIN ENTERPRISES LTD.

SWP-RLS

"GET AWAY FROM IT ALL"

Brand-new Subscribers-Only Sweepstakes

OFFICIAL ENTRY FORM

This entry must be received by: May 15, 1992
This month's winner will be notified by: May 31, 1992
Trip must be taken between: June 30, 1992—June 30, 1993

YES, I want to win the Canyon Ranch vacation for two. I understand the prize includes round-trip airfare and the two additional prizes revealed in the BONUS PRIZES insert.

Name _____

Address _____

City _____

State/Prov._____ Zip/Postal Code _____

Daytime phone number _____
(Area Code)

Return entries with invoice in envelope provided. Each book in this shipment has two entry coupons — and the more coupons you enter, the better your chances of winning!
© 1992 HARLEQUIN ENTERPRISES LTD.   2M-CPN